POLK GULCH

ANDREW BARDIN WILLIAMS

Polk Gulch
By Andrew Bardin Williams
eBook Edition: 978-0-4630-5475-8
Paperback Edition: 979-8-5256-1103-0
© Copyright 2020 Andrew Bardin Williams

CONTENTS

Chapter 1	1
Chapter 2	11
Chapter 3	17
Chapter 4	33
Chapter 5	39
Chapter 6	49
Chapter 7	55
Chapter 8	65
Chapter 9	75
Chapter 10	83
Chapter 11	93
Chapter 12	97
Chapter 13	101
Chapter 14	107
Chapter 15	115
Chapter 16	123
Chapter 17	129
Chapter 18	137
Chapter 19	149
Chapter 20	159
Thank you for Reading!	177
Learning to Haight	179
Also by Andrew Williams	189
About the Author	191

To Mom and Dad.

1

Wally brought the cheap beer up to his lips and took a small sip. He swallowed, letting the cool carbonated liquid burn his throat and warm his stomach, making him feel queer and safe at the same time. He leaned against the far wall, his back to the door, watching the band muddy their way through a bad Ramones cover. Wally cringed as the lead singer warbled through the chorus, playing to the group of half a dozen scantily-clad women at the foot of the stage, waving their arms in the air, groovin' to the music. A particularly skanky young woman who Wally guessed was barely legal drinking age stood directly in front and below the singer, her head upturned, eyes closed, mouthing the words to "I Wanna Be Sedated", half a beat behind the singer.

Wally stifled a laugh. The singer's theatrics and his naive, Twixter followers were just something true fans had to endure to appreciate the ironically horrific perfection of the group's live performances. Nothing more than an opening band, a tune-up to the main act, Mr. Roger's Coke Dealer played to the crowd, giving them what they wanted to hear, a few somewhat identifiable punk anthems before the real band came out on stage. They played their instruments loose and out of tune, keeping true to punk's we're-just-making-it-up-here mantra. They were playing a part, executing poorly played music that was part of a show, a caricature of what a punk band was supposed to be.

And Wally was fine with that. He'd been coming to Mr. Rogers shows for years, basically ever since he moved to San Francisco ten years ago. He'd happened into a bar on Polk Street late one night, a few beers in, having lost his friends between Vertigo and Kozy Kar. He'd heard the electric guitar chords and loud, steady beat from the sidewalk, and, tired of swaying and stumbling in and around the other drunken slobs, veered past the doorman and into the club.

The scene exploded in front of him that night as he made his way through the crowd toward the stage, slyly taking a mixed drink off a server's tray when she wasn't looking. At the time, Mr. Roger's Coke Dealer was still a college band from nearby Berkeley, and their fans reflected their punk sensibilities. The band fed off the crowd's energy, its angst, pushing the boundaries of what could be considered music. On average, their songs were just a minute long, played hectically and in a rush as if the band couldn't wait to turn the stage over to the headline act and join the violent throng thrashing around in front of them.

In true punk fashion, the band was made up of only three members, the sensitive lead singer and guitarist, the repressed bassist and a bad-ass female drummer who could have anyone she wanted in the whole damn bar. She absolutely owned the place and she knew it.

That night years ago, Wally drunkenly watched the

scene from his corner of the club, his eyes drawn to the drummer's frenetic energy, quiet confidence and omniscient stage presence. She had long brown hair tied back in a ponytail swishing to and fro as she hammered on her kit, a steel-studded dog collar around her neck. Wally fell in love that day, and he'd been coming to the band's shows ever since.

Now ten years later, the band was playing one of their originals, a high-energy raw song that compared suburban boredom to getting your eyes burned by hydrochloric acid. The bassist, a muscular man in his early thirties wearing leathers, was in the middle of his solo, the slow strumming pounding through the speakers as he basked in his time in the spotlight. He had half-inch wooden dowels in his ear lobes, stretching the skin like some ancient Amazon tribesman. Strobe lights and fractals pulsated in time to the beat, casting strange shadows on the three walls surrounding the stage and the audience. The band had come a long way in those ten years, Wally thought, noting that they had added stage production to their hectic, halting sound.

Wally focused past the bassist, to the back of the stage, fixating his gaze on the drummer behind, a pair of pink plastic shades pushed up on top of her head, the light reflecting in the lenses, her silhouette illuminated in fraction of a second intervals as the strobes did their thing. Her arms were a flurry, blurred against the backdrop on stage, her motion perfectly fluid. The only way the crowd could tell she was making contact with her kit was the hypnotic beat emanating over the small black box theater from her direction.

Faded jeans were just visible from behind her massive drum set, torn, tattered and held together by a series of safety pins and industrial staples. She wore a yellow Care Bears T-shirt and a brown leather choker around her slender neck. Her hair, tied back in a rockin' ponytail was held in place by a brown butterfly clip and the pair of pink sunglasses perched on her crown.

The crowd around Wally was getting thick, pinning him back against the bar, denim butts rubbing up against the front of his thighs. The throng in front of him was jumping in unison, timed to the baseline, each person with one arm outstretched, finger pointed at the band up on stage. A group of young hipsters, ironic T-shirts, fedora hats, shaggy haircuts, pogoed in the corner, jumping straight up with their arms pinned to their sides, crashing into each other as they stretched and elongated their bodies toward the ceiling in midflight.

Suddenly, the room had a closed, tight feeling. The crowd continued to press close, and Wally felt like he could scream at any moment. He'd been feeling more claustrophobic in public lately, fearful of tight crowds and small rooms, making sure to map out a route to open space if things got too cramped. Recently, he found himself checking for the emergency exits when entering a theater, a shopping mall or other large building, and he was going out less and less, content to stay home, curled up on the couch, his dog Joey huddled beneath the blanket draped over his body, the TV on, his mind at ease, safe.

The bass died down and the crowd opened up a bit as the band members floated on stage in slow motion, the last notes of the song eking out of their instruments. The crowd stopped jumping and erupted in cheers and shouts. A whoop went up, and Wally realized he also was shouting. Someone yelled "Freebird" and a collective chuckle replaced the catcalls.

The lead singer, wearing a faded black-leather jacket with chains connecting zipper to pocket, stepped up to the mic and nodded at the gaggle of girls in front of him. His hair was gelled into a tight mohawk--a fin running the length of his scalp from widow's peak to nape. He reached out and touched the fans' outstretched arms as each one shrieked louder and louder to be heard over her neighbor. The crowd quieted down as the singer opened his mouth to no doubt thank his fans for their support while he batted his eyelashes and shyly fumbled with his guitar strap.

Wally turned his gaze back to the drummer, having seen the band enough times to know that she was growing impatient with the lead singer's preening. It was an act--the singer's aloofness and the drummer's annoyance--but the dynamic worked, their rivalry just dopey drama made up on stage for their fans who were in on the joke. Sure enough, Wally saw a flash of movement as the drummer stood up, put her arms in the air and held aloft her drumsticks.

"We arrre Misssster Rogerrrr's Coke Dealer! And we're here to make sure you mutha' fuckers get high as fuck! One, two, three, four!" she yelled.

The crowd erupted as she struck her sticks together, setting the upcoming tempo. The other two band members scrambled into position, taking their cues from their drummer.

Boom, shish, boom, boom, shish went her beat as the bassist struggled to match her tempo. It took him a few seconds to catch up, but they were in sync by the fourth measure, and the singer soon joined in with the melody followed by the opening words.

Wally felt something brush against his shoulder, and he turned to see a man in his early twenties at his side at the bar air-guitaring to the song. He seemed out of place to Wally, his button-down shirt, perfectly coifed hair and right-fitting jeans giving him away. The man caught Wally's eye and smiled--only slightly embarrassed.

"Here to see Sunset Revolution?" Wally asked, referencing the headline act who would be going on after Mr. Roger's Coke Dealer.

The man nodded and picked up his pint glass.

"I never come for the opening band, but I thought I'd check it out." He shrugged as he shouted over the pulsating music. "These guys are quite a trip."

Wally wasn't surprised. He'd seen Mr. Roger's Coke Dealer open for Sunset Revolution dozens of times, and there was little overlap between fan bases. People like him had a name for these types--sunsetters.

Wally nodded back at the sunsetter and focused his attention back on the drummer and the rest of the group hamming it up on stage. The drummer's independent streak is what made her so great, Wally thought, why he loved her. She was the coolest cat he'd ever seen, her not-a-care-in-the-world attitude a refreshing contrast to his own depressed state. He was always afraid something bad was going to happen: a car crash, a stick-up gone wrong, a freakish accident that left him maimed, disabled for the rest of his life. He'd been having strange dreams lately of gruesome ways he could die or get hurt. A can of paint dropped on his head from a reckless contractor on some scaffolding. Getting sneezed on by someone with Ebola and his insides turning to mush. Falling from the fire escape of his Polk Gulch apartment building as he adjusted the satellite dish perched just out of reach.

Wally shook his head, trying fruitlessly to shake the paranoid thoughts. As he did, he noticed a dark stain above the right breast on his blue T-shirt. It was broth from the beef and broccoli soup he'd eaten before the show at Chai Yo, a noodle bar next door. In addition, his shirt was wrinkled, faded and frayed at the waist and his hair was a mess. He wasn't necessarily a slob, he just valued comfort and familiarity over style--in sharp contrast to the coiffed sunsetter next to him. Wally's appearance was even in contrast to that of the drummer he so admired who wore torn, out-of-date thrift store clothing but wore it well. She looked so cool, so confident in her skin, drumming frantically in front of hundreds of people, night after night in the trendiest clubs in the city. Who was he kidding?

The set over, Wally placed his Stella on the bar and watched the band begin to pack their equipment. The sunsetter next to him ordered another pint and pulled up a barstool to wait out the fifteen-minute intermission. The club started to empty of the punks who were slowly being replaced by the more modern, mainstream fans of Sunset Revolution.

"They're actually pretty good," the man said. Wally nodded, noticing that the statement reeked of condescension. He continued to watch the stage. A transformation was occurring, broken, beaten up instruments being replaced by newer equipment able to clean up the rough sound of live music for a force-fed fan base weaned on audiotuned music blasted out of iTunes, Pandora and iHeart radio.

The two sat in silence for a few minutes as roadies reset the stage and the bar filled up with more button-downs and golf shirts.

"I've been to at least half a dozen Sunset shows," the sunsetter next to him said, sipping his beer. "Best one was the Greek Theater in Berkeley. Great acoustics."

Wally raised his eyebrows. "Never seen Mr. Roger's Coke Dealer?"

The man laughed. "Is that their name? Good god. No, I never catch the opening act. What's the point? I'm always in the parking lot getting hammered. There's no parking lot in the middle of the city, so here I am. Glad I caught 'em though. They were rough but fun."

Cheers went through the crowd as the band took the stage and started making last minute sound checks. Wally motioned over his shoulder.

"You know they're the same band, right?"

The man looked confused.

"Sunset Revolution and Mister Roger's Coke Dealer. They're the same band."

The man swiveled around to face the stage, the puzzled expression frozen on his face. Wally swiveled with him.

"They're their own opening band. It's a goof."

The sunsetter stared at his favorite band, eyes narrowing, mouth slowly opening. The up-and-coming musicians with a Top-40 hit to their name were the same ones who'd just been wailing away in front of a much smaller crowd, purposely playing three-chord punk anthems with junked-up instruments slightly out of key--though they'd switched clothes and roles within the band. The bassist with the dowels in his ears was now the guitarist and lead singer--though he was now wearing tight designer jeans and a fitted black T-shirt. The drummer had changed into tight leather pants, fuck me boots and a sequined top, and she was now toting a long-necked bass guitar, the light reflecting off the shiny black paint job. The former lead singer was behind the drumkit, his mohawk washed out--an emo bedhead 'do making him slightly more presentable to the mothers in the audience. Each of them were now easily recognizable to the average US Weekly reader.

"No. Really?"

Wally nodded.

"Are you sure?"

He nodded again and picked up his beer, hiding a smug smile behind his pint glass.

"Well, I'll be damned. That's a fantastic idea."

Wally nodded a third time and continued to watch the stage, catching the eye of the drummer turned bassist. She stopped tuning her instrument and smiled back, brushing her bangs from her eyes, tucking them behind her ears. Wally's heart beat faster, even faster than the drummer's rhythmic beat, as she leapt off the stage, starting in his direction. She crossed half-way across the room before a good-looking hipster wearing a black tee and a fedora headed her off, pulling her aside. She halted, letting her body be diverted, but keeping her eyes fixated solely on Wally. Across the room, Wally frowned, his heart sank, his mind racing. Get real, he thought, falling back into his state of self-pity. She was too good for him, too beautiful, too hip. Too cool.

Wally watched her from afar, her head bobbing up and down in impatient agreement with the hipster. Her hand migrated down to her pocket where she pulled out a shiny platinum ring. She fumbled with it as the man kept talking, oblivious to her cues. Finally, she slipped the ring on her left hand, and quietly excused herself.

She turned back to Wally, and continued her walk through the crowd, waving to him as she neared. She stumbled as she walked, clearly uncomfortable in her stage clothes. Wally left the sunsetter agape on his barstool as he took a step forward, meeting her mid stride. He gave her a sheepish hug, pulling her in tight, trying to engulf her in his arms, hoping he could keep her there the rest of the night.

"Great show tonight," he whispered in her ear.

The woman wriggled free. "We haven't even gone on yet."

"You know I like the opening band best. And I know you do too. You guys were great."

"I dunno. Were we? Xander was a little too schmaltzy."

"Well that's part of the show, isn't it?"

"I guess, but I wanted to just push on through, you know?"

Wally shrugged. "It was a good show, sweetie. And the next set is going to be great."

The drummer smiled. "And you're a great husband, Wally. Thanks for coming." She gave him a slight squeeze around his waist.

"Wouldn't miss it for the world, Jules. I wouldn't miss it for the world." And right then and there, they both knew that he meant it.

2

The fog streamed up and over the lip of the cliff like a mountain stream running over moss-covered rocks. The coastal airstream hit the rock face, lifting the moisture over the seventy-five-foot wall and back down the other side. Wally's feet and legs were shrouded up to his knees, invisible, making him wonder if they were still there.

Julie was up ahead of him, skipping gaily in spite of the large drop-off on each side of the hiking trail. Wally held up, unsure of his footing, sweat streaking down his temples and jawline, collecting at the end of his pointy chin. He wanted to call out, to order Julie to halt. They needed to turn back. The risk was not worth the reward. But his voice was hoarse, he'd been singing too loud to KFOG on the ride over the Golden Gate Bridge. His words leaked out of his mouth and were swallowed up by the fog, dropping out of the air a few feet from his position.

Suddenly, a dark shape to his right caught his attention. A bird fighting the upcurrent whipped over the lip of the cliff, narrowly missing Wally. The avian continued over the ridge-

line on its way inland as Wally lurched to his left, losing his balance, leaning dangerously close to falling off the trail down the leeward side of the slope. He over-compensated however, and his body listed the other way, toward the ocean and the seventy-five foot drop to the jagged rocks and crashing waves below. He waved his arms to catch himself, but it was too late. His heart rose into his chest as the image of Julie's face, masked in horror, shrunk in front of him as he fell...

"You awake?" Wally whispered.

Julie mumbled and turned over, facing the wall. She pulled the light blue duvet up around her shoulders, covering any exposed skin. Her brown hair was mussed, uncombed, wildly strewn about the pillow, tangled. Wally could see a crease in her locks signifying where she'd worn a scrunchy the night before, and her stage makeup was still on, smeared across her temple and cheek like a Cherokee warrior in a bad spaghetti western. Light was beginning to peek through the drawn shades, streaks of sunshine running the length of their bedroom's hardwood floors.

"I had another bad dream."

Julie stirred once again and reached back under the covers, gingerly sliding her hand between Wally's legs. Her skin was cool compared to his, and she rubbed his lower thighs just above his knobby knees.

"We were hiking on the ridgeline above Tennessee Valley and a big bird knocked me off the cliff."

"Oh yeah?" Her hand started to migrate north toward his crotch. "How big?"

Wally separated his knees, an invitation to continue.

"Big enough."

"Was it yellow?"

"Yellow? What? No. It was black, I guess."

"Was it reciting the ABCs?"

Wally snapped his legs shut.

"Not funny."

Julie giggled, her hand trapped tightly between Wally's legs.

"Was Mr. Hooper there? Did you see the Snuffleupagus?"

"Ok, now you've done it." Still trapping Julie's hand with his thighs, he pivoted in bed, rolling over her wrist and arm, ending up in her embrace, face-to-face, one arm beneath his body, the other draped on top.

Julie laughed, snuggling close, squeezing him tightly. Her hair cascaded over her face, hiding her eyes, only the tip of her nose poking through the tangled strands. Wally felt her breath on his chest--it was hot and sticky--and she smelled like stale beer from the club, but he didn't mind.

"It means nothing," she said. "It's just a dream."

Wally took a deep breath. He knew it wasn't just a dream. It was something more, more sinister than just his runaway imagination. He was scared, but how could he explain that to the woman he loved, someone he was supposed to protect, keep secure? He was supposed to chase her dreams away, not the other way around.

But he had to at least pretend.

They lay there, motionless, silent, content to be in each other's arms for a few minutes as they delayed the start of their day as long as they could. Wally ticked off all that they had to do. They were meeting the band for breakfast and then heading over to the studio to meet with an executive from Apple who wanted to feature Sunset Revolution in their next iPhone ad. Potey, the band's manager, told them the tech company liked to feature up-and-coming bands who were on the cusp of breaking out--an effort to be seen as a hip, trendsetting brand. Sunset Revolution had just scored their first Top-40 hit, and their upcoming album was generating a lot of buzz among critics. Potey promised that the iPhone spot would guarantee a choice spot at one of the summer music festivals. The Warped Tour, Coachella, maybe even Bonnaroo. After that? Who knew?

Following the meeting with Apple, Potey would then want to go over last night's show. They'd take taxis to Land's End for a photo shoot for some press material, and then it was dinner with some friends.

Julie exhaled slowly on Wally's chest while his short, choppy breaths ruffled the bangs covering her face.

"I don't like that you take off your wedding ring during shows," he said after a few minutes.

Julie nuzzled closer into his chest. He could feel the skin around her jaw tighten, a sign that she was smiling.

"You give all those creepy fans of yours false hope."

"False hope?" she teased, emphasizing false. Her voice was muffled as it emanated off Wally's warm body. Wally exhaled, shaking his head. "Come on, baby. You know I can't play with it on. It irritates my skin."

"I know, but I don't have to like it."

A few more minutes passed, and Wally slowly extricated himself from Julie's arms and sat up on the bed. He rubbed his eyes and popped his daily anti-depressant with a glass of water that Julie had put out for him the night before. He then stood up, moved to the kitchen and started the coffee. In a few minutes, he returned with a small glass of orange juice.

"Here's your liquid sunshine, Jules."

Julie yawned and stretched under the blankets, her arms extending to the four corners of the bed like a starfish. Propping herself up on her elbow, she took the glass from Wally and took a gulp. Her eyes, previously squinty, unwilling to let in the growing light, suddenly opened wide. She let out a satisfying sigh, a sound Wally recognized as the same sound she let out when she reached orgasm.

"Orange juice is so good," she said, smacking her lips. "It really wakes you up in the morning."

Wally laughed, taking the glass out of her hand.

"I told you, it's liquid sunshine straight from the heavens."

"And where do you get this magic liquid?"

"I know a guy. Short fellow. Green hair, googily eyes."

"Oh yeah? How'd you meet this creature?"

"Grindr."

Julie laughed. "He must have met Vacation Wally then. Work Wally would never join Grindr. Too risky."

"Vacation Wally does like to take chances," Wally said, referencing himself in the third-person. "But then it's back to boring, paranoid, self-depreciating Work Wally once he walks back through security at SFO."

"I like both Vacation and Work Wally," Julie responded, tilting her head to the side as if she were flirting. "Each comes with its benefits."

"Right. Vacation Wally is adventurous. Work Wally pays the bills and makes sure the door is deadbolted every night before we go to sleep."

"Listen, buddy. I became enamored with Vacation Wally but fell in love with Work Wally."

"It's our charm."

"I guess I should hold onto you then. For the liquid sunshine hookup, of course."

"It would be in your best interest."

Julie swung her legs around and sat up straight.

"I'll keep you as long as you take out the dog. He's crossing his legs."

Wally turned around to see Joey, their Boston Terrier sitting on his haunches in the middle of their bedroom, his eyes fixated squarely on Wally, his tail brushing the floor behind him.

"Come on, buddy. Let's empty your bowels," Wally said, grabbing a pair of pants draped over a chair in the corner of the room. "The diva wants to sleep in, and we're going to let her."

"Thanks honey," Julie said as she dived back under the duvet. "Maybe we can take him to the beach later for the photoshoot?"

"Sure."

"We can get some more shells for the garden."

Wally nodded and smiled as he gathered the dog's leash and a poo bag. "Don't get too comfortable," he said as he opened the door. "We're having amazing sex when I get back."

The outline of her body curled up on her side in the fetal position was the last thing he saw as he closed the door behind him.

3

"E."

"N."

"I."

Wally paused, looking around the room at his friends. Three teams of two sat around a dining room table in a posh flat on Union Street in the Marina district. The apartment belonged to Annette and Geoff, two friends who had grown up with Julie in nearby Antioch and had gotten married shortly after graduation. Geoff had just sold his startup to Google--something to do with cloud security--and the apartment was the couple's first extravagant spend.

A game, Cranium, was laid out on the table in front of them, color-coded playing pieces scattered at various stages on the board. Because of a little-talked about incident, couples were barred from playing together, so Wally was paired up with Julie's manager Potey, and the two men were taking turns calling out letters, trying to spell a word backwards.

"Can you pronounce it again?" Wally asked, feeling everyone's eyes on him.

"Sang-gwin," thirty-two year old, red-haired and Berkeley educated Abby enunciated. She squinted as she read the card, crow's feet forming around her eyes. "It means sunny, optimistic, hopeful."

"Everything you're not," Julie teased. She winked when Wally threw her a glance, and Potey impatiently urged him to continue.

Acting as Julie's band manager for just a few years, Potey and Wally had grown close, Potey's blue-collar Boston accent a fixture at their dinner parties and game nights. He'd rarely come solo to these events, dragging along a string of young ladies, caked with too much makeup and too little clothing. Sometimes the group would see a woman two or three times, but more often than not, it was one time and done. Tonight however, Potey was alone.

Born Dan Poteet, Potey was a stocky, cocky ladies' man. The first time Wally had met Potey was at a Sunset Revolution show in Oakland. Wally and Julie had just gotten married, and the band was just starting to show signs of future success. Their single had started to get air time on local radio and a video they launched on YouTube was getting some attention. Potey had approached the band after one of their shows, and they had decided to give him a shot as their manager. At the time, Wally had found it odd that Potey was wearing a sports coat over a polo shirt--like an extra in the Eighties TV show Miami Vice--at a grungy concert venue, a place that had once hosted the Sex Pistols on their only North American tour. Everyone else was wearing casual clothes, mostly denim with some leathers mixed in. Potey seemed oblivious. Other people who were over or inappropriately dressed would have tried to blend in the background, hide in a corner, at least keep quiet to keep the attention from their wardrobe choices. Not Potey. Eager to make an impression with the musicians, the former high-tech PR executive stood at the bar, introducing himself to everyone who happened by, getting drinks for the band members and talking loudly with the bartender. That night he ended up buying Wally a Manhattan--seriously, at an underground rock club!--and started calling him Wall-ster, Wal-rus, Walton, Wal-seph and any other derivative of his given name. Since then the nicknames had never stopped.

"Come on, Walt the Fault," Potey exclaimed now. "We've got this. Sanguine. E-N-I."

Wally wrinkled his nose. English wasn't his best subject, but Potey had claimed to have been a communications major once upon a time and insisted they stick to Cranium's verbal categories rather than the logic questions that Wally usually got right.

"Sang-gwin." Wally pronounced. He paused then settled on his next letter. "U."

A groan went up from the other teams.

"We thought we had you there."

"Quiet, please," insisted Potey, in his thick New England accent. "We're still goin' here. G."

"N."

"A."

"S."

"Boom, motherfuckers!" Potey lept up from the table and slapped Wally five. He turned and let out a whoop in one of the other player's face before settling back down. Wally smirked and passed him the dice as Potey ran his fingers through his slicked-back hair.

"We're on a roll, bitches!"

"Potey, please," pleaded Annette, the hostess. "Sandy is sleeping."

"Sorry, sorry. Just gettin' a little excited here. Me and Wall Street are kickin' some ass."

"Well, try to contain your exuberance," came the response, this time form Annette's husband, Geoff, who was the one who had just gotten a face-full from Potey. There was a sound of footsteps coming down the hall, the pit-pattering echoing off the glossy hardwood floors and bare walls of the three-bedroom apartment.

"Damnit, Potey. I just got her to lie down," Annette said.

Wally's eyes met Julie's from across the table as Potey shrugged and moved his and Wally's game piece a few more spaces toward the center of the board. Julie smiled, and Wally made a face.

Annette sighed, pushing her Vodka and Tonic toward the center of the table, and stood up. Her curly hair was normally a mess, a casualty of motherhood, but tonight it was obvious she had spent extra time doing it up. Long brown locks on the side of her head that normally were left wild were combed and straightened and tucked behind her ears. She was wearing a nice, trendy top that was tapered in all the right places, and the "errands jeans" that she usually wore were replaced by pressed slacks. Put a pen behind her ear, and she'd look like she still did the books for Geoff's startup. A part of the team from the beginning, she became a jack-of-all-trades for the company, running marketing, sales and accounting at various stages until employees with the appropriate experience could be hired. She even did a little coding at one point.

"I got it," Julie said, putting her hand on Annette's arm. "I'll put her down for you."

Annette paused, looking back and forth between the open hallway door and her Vodka Tonic.

"Thanks, Julie," she said and sat down.

Wally watched as Julie pushed her chair back and exited the room. He could hear her muffled voice speak in sing-song fashion, no doubt trying to coax little Sandy back to her room. He heard a rustling sound and then Julie's heavier footsteps fade away.

Wally arched his eyebrows, turning his attention back to the game. Potey was reading a card aloud to Geoff, who was holding a mound of clay that he would have to mold into a mystery object for his partner--Pictionary for the 3D generation.

"She's great with kids, isn't she?" Abby said. She was seated next to Wally, holding a wine glass, her cheeks flushed and her lips stained red.

"You think so?" Wally responded, picking up his own drink.

"I know so. We used to tag team on babysitting jobs back in college. She was the responsible one."

The thought of a twenty-year-old Jules all punked out in her leathers, dyed hair and torn, tattered jeans watching over some Berkeley professor's snotty kid made him laugh.

"If she was the responsible one, what did that make you?"

Abby thought for a second. "I was the front," she decided. "I'd put on a nice floral dress, comb my hair and make nice for the parents. Jules did all the work."

Wally hated it when other people called his wife by her nickname. He'd started using it shortly before they got engaged seven years earlier, and her friends had picked up on it recently. It made him feel that they were intruding on their domestic life, using his nickname for her that should have been just between them.

"When are you guys going to pop one out?" Abby asked, smirking.

Geoff was hurriedly working with the molding clay across the table. He had rolled out four worm-like pieces and was now working on a sphere with the rest. Wally ignored Abby's question and leaned forward, feigning interest in the masterpiece in the making.

"Come on," Abby pressured, setting her wine glass on the table. She brushed away her red hair from her shoulder and leaned in. "I won't tell anyone."

Wally could smell the wine on her breath. It was sour and warm but with a hint of fruit. Abby's mouth was curved up into a sly smile, like she was transported back to her freshman dorm, and she was trying to find out this upperclassman's true feelings for her roommate. It was cute and showed that Abby really cared about Julie. Regardless, Wally didn't want to tell her his secret, the conversation he'd had with Julie just a few days before.

Like Abby, Julie wanted to know when they would start trying to have a baby. They'd been married for six years, longer than most of their friends who were already starting families. Wally would be turning thirty-three in a few months, and Julie was nearing thirty-two. Wally was making good money at his sales job at a technology company downtown. Sunset Revolution was on the verge of stardom--Potey had seen to that--and what was cooler than a chick bass player other than a pregnant bass player?

"We haven't talked about it," Wally lied.

"Bullshit." Abby picked up her wine glass and shook it in Wally's face. "Bullshit."

"What's bullshit?" Potey asked. Some people had gaydar. Potey claimed to have drama-dar, the ability to sense conflict.

"Nothing."

"Wally says that he and Jules haven't even talked about having a kid."

"I don't--"

"Yep, I'm calling bullshit, too," Annette interrupted. She turned her attention away from Geoff's clay creation and continued, "She tells us all the time how she wants to start trying."

"Hey, are you guys paying attention? I'm creating here." Geoff said as he continued to work away at the clay. But the others had turned their attention to Wally.

Wally cringed, taken aback by the sudden turn in conversation. All eyes were on him as he scanned the dining room, his gaze washing over the wine rack under the window, the china cabinet under a large mirror and hanging on the far wall, a slightly blurry photograph that Geoff had taken of Vernal Falls in Yosemite.

"Are you guys harassing my husband?" Julie asked as she walked back into the room, an amused look on her face. She stopped just inside the doorway and put her hands on her hips. "You can't do that. He's a timid little creature." Potey and Geoff laughed as Julie reached out to ruffle Wally's short-cropped hair. She teased, "You can't talk about scary things like children or you'll scare him back into his little hole."

"Your time's running out," Wally blurted to Geoff, eyeing the plastic hourglass, hoping to end the conversation. Instead, Geoff shrugged and put his arm around Annette, leaning back in his chair, letting the conversation continue.

"Wally said you guys haven't talked about having kids," Potey summarized for Julie.

"Annette and I called bullshit," Abby added.

"Well, is it?" asked Annette.

Julie cocked her head to the side as she smiled at Wally. Their eyes met from across the table, she standing, he trapped in his seat between Abby and Potey. She wasn't performing tonight, so her hair was down and straight, reaching just below the tops of her shoulders. She was wearing a T-shirt and jeans, though the jeans weren't ripped and the shirt didn't feature any cartoon characters on it--just plain yellow with a small breast pocket. As he fumbled with the plastic hourglass, Wally imagined that Julie was probing him, trying to gauge whether it was worth having this conversation in front of their friends.

"Wally thinks he's going to die," she said.

Annette gasped.

"Are you sick?" Abby asked.

Wally sighed, lowering his eyes to the table. He really didn't want to have this conversation--not in front of these people.

"No. I'm not sick. I just have a feeling, I guess."

"What kind of feeling?" Geoff had put aside the clay and was leaning forward across the table.

"I just know that I'm going to die young."

"What do you mean, you know you're going to die young?" Potey asked, his face contorted in a half sneer, half scowl. "How do you know that?"

Julie pulled out a chair and sat down. Abby and Annette looked to her to fill in the gaps, but her face gave nothing away. She was smiling, looking amused.

"Wally thinks he's going to pass away before he turns forty," Julie said.

Abby flinched. "And you don't want to have kids because you won't be around to help raise them?"

"Something like that," Wally said as he continued looking down at the board in front of him, his and Potey's playpiece much further along than the others.

"Wait, wait, wait." Potey stood up, pushing his chair behind him with the back of his thighs. The legs slid across the hardwood floors, making a horrible scratching sound. Annette craned her neck to inspect the damage. "This is insane."

Wally sighed. "I can't explain it, but that's how I feel. I've always known." He looked across the table at Julie who had sat back down, calm, her arms crossed, content to let the group shame her husband into submission. Wally wouldn't be swayed, though, he'd had this feeling his entire life, and his recent dreams were simply a validation that his time on earth was coming to a close.

"Why don't you just get life insurance?" offered Geoff. "You get a ten- or twenty- year policy and by then your long-term planning will be in place. You make good money. Your family will be taken care of."

"Finance is only part of the equation. It's playing catch in the backyard. It's teaching him to ride a bike. Helping her with homework. Picking out his first car. Driving her to college."

"Your kid will still experience all that. Just not with you." Annette said, her eyebrows scrunched together in a scowl. "We'd all be there to help Jules."

"I'd be there," Potey offered.

"That's what I'm afraid of." Wally allowed himself a smile, but it was short-lived.

"This is nuts. You're not going to die," exclaimed Annette. "Why are we talking about this?"

"What about Jules?" Abby motioned at Julie across the table, ignoring Annette's plea to change the subject. "Whether you have a kid or not, you'd be leaving Julie in the lurch. What's the difference?"

Wally's heart sunk. Of course, he'd thought of that. Julie, however, answered for him.

"He's picked out a mate for me."

"Oh, God," Geoff gasped. Annette opened her mouth, her tongue visible behind her teeth, flexed and pointed, ready but unwilling to form words. Finally, she turned to Wally.

"What the fuck is wrong with you?"

"Relax, guys. It's not as bad as it seems. If something terrible happens to me I'd want Jules to move on and be with someone who'd treat her as I'd treat her."

"How chivalrous." Annette was having trouble hiding her disdain. Geoff put his arm around her and gave her shoulder a pat, an apparent attempt to calm her down.

"How do you pick someone?" Abby seemed more curious than angry or disappointed. "I mean, is it someone we know? Please tell me it's not Potey."

"I would be happy to do your husbandly duty, Wally. Just let me know when and where."

Wally shook his head. "The person knows. That's all that matters."

Potey snorted. "I can just imagine the ad you posted on Craigslist. Wanted. Future husband for sloppy seconds. Must live up to enormous responsibility. Small penis preferred."

"There was a bit more of a vetting process than that." Wally leaned back, his gaze climbing up the dining room wall in front of him, avoiding eye contact with anyone, hoping the conversation was over. The rest of the group looked at each other, shaking their heads, taking deep breaths as if they were trying to take it all in. Even Potey was at a loss of words. Finally, Abby broke the silence.

"How do you think you're going to die?"

"I don't know," Wally said, shrugging.

"It's going to be spectacular," chimed in Julie. It was the first thing she'd said in several minutes.

Wally shrugged again.

"Ok. I'm just trying to wrap my head around this," Geoff chimed in. "What are you doing to prepare for this-- for this-- inevitability?"

"Let me answer that." A smirk washed over Julie's face. "Let's see, we have a really expensive life insurance policy--"

"How much?" Potey interrupted.

"Two million dollars," Wally sheepishly answered. He hung his head low.

"Shit," Geoff said. Potey whistled.

"All the bills are in my name--" Julie continued.

"--So she doesn't have to change them all over when I'm gone. That's such a pain--"

"--P, G and E. Comcast. Health insurance premium. Even our Netflix account--"

"--She'll need to continue to stream movies--"

"--And the car is in my name--"

"--the DMV is such a nightmare--"

"--Funeral arrangements are already made--"

"--I want to be cremated and scattered in the Bay. Maybe a brass band playing some old New Orleans song in the background. I want people to celebrate, you know?"

Wally looked up and noticed that the others were starting to smile.

"He's even recorded a video to play on his Facebook page from beyond the grave."

Potey and Abby chuckled, and elbowed each other in the ribs. Geoff shook his head.

"You're sick, you know that?" Annette's voice was still tinged with anger, but at least she was smiling.

"Yeah, I know I'm sick. But it's who I am."

Hours later, Wally and Julie stumbled out of Geoff's and Annette's walkup, buzzed from the wine and conversation. It was past midnight, and they turned toward Broadway and their apartment on Polk Street--the steep street grid that made up Pac Heights between them. It would be a difficult walk. Up on the hill above them, stately, post-earthquake mansions and luxury apartment buildings loomed, all with great views, but not the easiest neighborhood to walk through.

They'd lived on Polk Street in the valley between Nob Hill and Pacific Heights since they were married, Julie letting

Wally pick it out after the two of them lived during their year-long engagement in a run-down flat in the Haight, just blocks from the famous Haight-Ashbury street sign. It had been a musician's apartment, messy, various instruments strewn about, shared with other band mates who slept all day and played all night. Wally, the only one in the building with a traditional nine-to-five, finally convinced Julie to move to nicer digs. She agreed, but with the caveat they get a dog to keep her company while Wally was at work. A Boston terrier, she named him Joey after the front man for the Ramones.

"Sorry about putting you on the spot back there," Julie said as they began their climb.

Wally shrugged and continued walking. Even though the conversation ended amicably, he wasn't thrilled with his wife airing their dirty laundry in front of their friends. Potey would never let him live it down, and he was pretty sure that Annette hated him. He considered scolding Julie, at least telling her how he felt, but her stumbles and swaying motion as they walked told him he had best wait until they had sobered up.

"I joke about this fascination you have about dying, but it really bothers me," Julie continued. "It's hard being with someone who doesn't think we're going to have a future together."

Wally opened his mouth to protest, but Julie interrupted.

"I know, I know. The lack of commitment in your mind isn't voluntary. But it has the same effect. I need to be with someone who is confident he's going to be around long term. It's shitty."

Wally shut his eyes tight as they walked side-by-side, mentally urging her to drop the conversation.

"This is the part where you reassure me," Julie said. "Do you not want to talk about it?"

Wally stopped, turning his body to face his wife. They were half-way up the block under a street lamp in front of a three-story white apartment building. An awning covered the front entryway where a call box listed the tenants' apartment numbers. Wally took her hand in his and looked deep into her eyes.

"I'm sorry I can't change the way that I feel. I'm always going to have that feeling," he said.

Julie's face fell. She looked at the patch of sidewalk between them and a crack as wide and deep as their positions. Wally's heart sank. He hated seeing her sad. He wanted to please her, to give her everything she ever wanted. He'd kill for her.

"Listing it all out like that sounded ridiculous, didn't it," Wally admitted. "Maybe I am crazy." Continuing to hold her hand, he started up the hill again toward home. The warmth and emotion left Julie's hand, laying there in his, cold, clammy, unfeeling.

They continued to walk hand-in-hand, stoically up the hill as Wally began singing. "I... am one of those. Mella-dramatic fools. Neuro-tic to the bone, no doubt about it." Julie remained silent. "Sometimes I give myself the-uh creeps. Sometimes my mind plays tricks ah-on me." Again, nothing from his wife. "It all keeps adding up. I think I'm cracking uh-up. Am I just paranoid? Am I just stoooooned?"

"Are you seriously quoting Green Day lyrics to me right now?"

"Maybe. Is it working?"

Warily, Wally looked at Julie out of the corner of his eye,

but she was smiling, dimples exposed, ruddy cheeks glistening under the street lamps. He smiled back and squeezed her hand, and he knew that she knew she had him. They took another couple of steps before she finally sang.

"I-uh went to a shrink. To analyze my dreams. He said it's lack of sex that keepin' meeeee down." Julie raised her voice and began shouting the song. "I-uh went to a whore. He said my life's a bore. It's my lack of sex that's keepin' hiiim down."

Julie reached out and held onto a streetlight, pirouetting around it with Wally in tow. After a full revolution she stopped and pulled him in close.

"You're not going anywhere. Ok? We're going to be together a long time. No one is ever going to see that morbid Facebook video you recorded." She paused to catch her breath. Wally stood there in her arms, half-way up the steep block, the two holding each other around their waists, making intense eye contact. "I want to have a baby with you, Walter Drummond. Badly. I want it to have my eyes and your chin."

"I do have a chiseled chin."

"The best chin."

"But what's wrong with my eyes?"

Julie let go of his waist, turned ninety degrees and slid her arm around the crook of his elbow, inserting her hand into his front jeans pocket. They walked in silence for a block, arm in arm, breathing quietly as they walked up toward the crest of the hill.

4

Wally lay in bed flat on his back, the covers up to his chin. He stared up at the ceiling, cracked plaster running the length of their bedroom. He could hear muffled talking from just outside the door. It was Julie, whispering softly, haltingly with someone with a much deeper voice. Everything in the room was still, and he couldn't move his head or anything else for that matter. It felt like he didn't have a body or a face. It was just his brain and his eyes, staring straight up at the ceiling. Just then, the realization hit him. He was paralyzed. He'd never walk again. A vegetable. A worthless, shitty vegetable that would forever be a burden on his young, energetic wife. He wanted to die.

Something was poking him in the back. Hard. Wally lifted his head and peered over his shoulder. Julie, her eyes round and wide stared back at him, mischief bubbling up from inside her. He turned over, yawned and stretched, taking note of every body part from his toes to the strands of his hair to make sure they were still there and functioning properly. Julie was poking him with her index finger under the sheets, waiting impatiently for him to wake.

"Morning, sleepy," she said, placing her hand on Wally's stomach. "Whatcha thinkin' about?"

"You, of course."

"I want to talk about last night."

Wally turned so he was on his side, facing his wife. She was perched up on her elbow towering above him. He looked up, softening his gaze.

"Ok. Go ahead."

"I'm sorry everyone ganged up on you, including me."

Wally propped himself up with his right arm and rubbed his eyes with his free hand. He nodded.

"I just really want to build a family with you. I think we're ready."

"Maybe I am being silly. I love you. You love me. We're in a good place." Julie smiled as Wally continued. "Maybe I'm just happy with our relationship as it is. I like that it's just us two." He paused. "And Joey of course."

Julie reached behind her and pressed a button on their alarm clock sitting on a nightstand. An acoustic version of a David Grey song flowed out of the speakers. "Are you always going to feel that way? I mean, is this it?"

Wally sighed, scrunching his face in the process. The room was dimly lit with the shades drawn but a few streaks of sunlight slipped in around the sides of the windows. He looked down at the mattress between them. A wrinkle in the fitted sheet ran between them from Wally's bare nipple to Julie's T-shirt covered stomach. From his perspective, Wally imagined it as a long, narrow mountain range running across a flat dessert plateau. He wanted to take a few moments to think about his answer, knowing full well that this was it.

He opened his mouth with the intention of affirming Julie's suspicions, but the words got caught in his throat. Soundless air escaped, whistling past his teeth and out into the expanse of the bedroom. Panic spread throughout his body as his pulse and breathing increased and he grew light-headed. He tried to swallow but his mouth was dry. He puffed out his chest, hoping to force out the words he wanted to say.

Wally burped softly and, surprised, quickly clapped his hand over his mouth. Julie's eyes grew wide, and she burst out laughing, arching her neck and head back so Wally could see up her pulsating nostrils. Her roar filled the gaping space between them as she reached her hand out and teasingly pushed Wally's face so he flopped onto his back. He giggled and reached out to tickle his wife. She writhed around under the covers, fighting to keep Wally's hands from touching her soft skin, her boisterous laugh never ceasing.

After a few minutes they calmed down, gasping for breath, arms intertwined, embracing and squeezing each other. Wally's knee was crammed between Julie's thighs, and her leg was draped over his hip. They lay there, breathing heavily, listening to each other's silence as if reorganizing their thoughts.

"Wally?" Julie finally said.

"Jules?"

"Something is missing. If you die--and I want to make that clear--if you die, I'd love to have your baby there to comfort me and to remind me of you when you're gone. I want to look into its eyes and see a piece of you. I want to tell stories about how kind you are, how funny you can be. How adventurous when you get out of your own head. I want to describe our wonderful life together. If I can't grow old with you, I want to grow old with your offspring, raising him--or her--to be as special and as caring of a person as you. Please do this for me."

Wally shifted his position in the bed, grabbing Julie's leg under her knee and pulling her closer to him. Their stomachs pressed together and her face mashed into his chest. He closed his eyes and reopened them.

"Yes," he said. "Let's do it."

"Seriously?" Julie's voice was muffled, but Wally could tell she was smiling.

"You convinced me. I want to give you everything you need."

Julie pulled her face out from the crevice of Wally's chest, a tear rolling down her cheek.

"You make me so happy," she said.

"You make me so happy," he repeated.

"I love you."

"I love you, too."

They lay in silence for a few more minutes, holding each other. Wally softly stroked Julie's bare arm, and she in turn squeezed Wally's butt. Eventually, their gentle caresses turned more passionate.

"I guess we're starting now," cooed Julie as Wally started to kiss her neck. "I'll have to throw out my pills."

Wally reached over to the couple's dresser while continuing to kiss Julie. He fumbled around until he found the brass handle on the top drawer and pulled it open. After searching around for a few moments with his hand--while continuing to explore Julie's body--he pulled out her birth control packet, thirty color-coded tablets sealed in plastic. Wally threw the packet across the room where it bounced against a floor lamp by the window and narrowly missed the dog bed where Joey was softly snoring.

Julie groaned as Wally pulled down her pajama pants, running his palms over her course pubic hair. He cupped her crotch and inserted a finger into her moist slit as she arched her back, urging him in deeper.

"You know," Wally whispered in her ear as he started a circular motion with his finger. "I read somewhere that giving head before sex increases the chance of conception. Something to do with the sperm count--"

"Shut up and put it inside me." Julie gasped as she pulled off Wally's boxers and grabbed his penis with both hands. "Put it inside me and fill me up with your juice."

Wally laughed, wriggled his butt so his boxers fell down to his knees and gave her what she wanted, the clock radio serenading them as they did their best to create a new life.

5

The fluorescent lighting made everything seem blue. The uncomfortable chairs. The pile of months old magazines. The vending machines. The long hallway. The gurney lining the walls. The nurses' scrubs.

Wally was in a daze, like he was high on cold medicine. He was aware of things happening around him, but he was detached, watching from above as his head floated up to the ceiling, separated from reality. Potey was across from him, fruitlessly trying to read ESPN The Magazine, Abby next to Potey, her eyes red from crying. Next to Wally were Geoff and Annette, holding hands. Geoff's head was upturned and his eyes were closed while Annette stared straight ahead, expressionless, the color drained from her face.

Wally suddenly became aware he was dreaming his own demise. His friends were in a hospital waiting room, worried he wouldn't make it, each dealing with potential loss in their own weird way. It was strange looking in on the scene, the time and place where his end was near. Wally wondered how he had passed. A high-speed car accident? Was it cancer? Had he gone quickly or did he suffer? Was he lying in a hospital bed down the hall at this moment or was he already gone, his soul slowly making its way through the waiting room on its way to…where?

"Mr. Drummond? Walter Drummond?" A booming voice interrupted his train of thought. Wally looked up and noticed a doctor in a white coat, stethoscope hanging around his neck, tongue depressor in his front shirt pocket. He was looking directly at Wally. Geoff nudged Wally, motioning for him to stand. He helped him up and gently guided him toward the doctor patiently waiting at the edge of the waiting room. The detached feeling was suddenly gone and Wally was aware of his legs moving, though he still felt like he was on autopilot, drifting toward his fate. His feet kept going, one step at a time, one after the other, closer and closer to the doctor.

The man put his arm around Wally and turned him around so that Wally was now facing his friends, still sitting yards away, each one looking up anxiously and fearful. Something wasn't right.

The doctor said some words but Wally couldn't hear. His ears rang then went deaf, the world suddenly blank, free of sound, color and meaning.

Wally started to swoon, and the doctor caught his arm. He motioned at an orderly standing by with a wheelchair, and the two slowly set him down. Over the doctor's shoulder, Wally saw Abby's face contort, her mouth open like she was screaming. Her mouth was wide and black, her uvula hanging and vibrating in the void. It must have been loud because people rushed to her side, but Wally heard nothing, like he was in a vacuum, floating through the scene, a fly on the wall, observing, watching.

He looked down at his hands in his lap. They were shaking uncontrollably. The doctor knelt down to ask him a question, but Wally didn't understand. What was going on? Where was Jules? This is a dream, right? Right?

Wally stared at the bottle in front of him, slouched in his chair, shoulders drooped, his eyes glazed over, alone in his apartment. He'd wanted to go out and get a bottle of Jack Daniels or some sort of vodka, a nice tequila perhaps, but he couldn't muster the energy to leave the apartment. He'd found a half-empty bottle of brandy in a kitchen cabinet where they stored their pots and pans. He wasn't sure where it came from, though he thought that maybe Julie had used it for cooking.

His heart beating fast, Wally picked up the bottle, turning it over in his hands. It was heavy and an odd oblong shape. The label, silver with gold trimming, read "E&J Rare Blend, Original, Extra, Smooth" in maroon lettering. He unscrewed the cap and took a whiff. His nostrils flared and burned at the boozy, medicinal odor, and he quickly turned his head away.

His eyes caught a large glass vase on the windowsill filled with a variety of seashells and smoothly worn rocks. He'd spent months emptying his pockets of items he'd found washed up on shore during walks with Joey along Chrissy Beach near the Marina. At least twice a week he'd let the dog off leash and let him romp around in the sand, penned in by the crystal cold water of San Francisco Bay on their right and marine wildlife protected sand dunes on their left. Joey could go straight for a mile and a half from the parking lot before they were turned away by a fence protecting a wildlife sanctuary. Along the way, Wally would pocket a silver dollar or a tiny conch, maybe a piece of granite that had been washed up on shore and worn smooth from centuries in the water--items that he'd deposit in the vase upon his return. Julie planned to one day use them as flowerbed coverings for their first home, when they finally got their act together and purchased a house, their own little piece of the city there in the suburbs.

Wally squeezed his eyes tight, brought the bottle to his lips and tilted his head back. The liquor hit his puckered lips, burning the skin before he parted them and gulped. Wally coughed, spraying the brandy across the white plaster wall of his living room. He gagged and slammed the bottle on the table, bending at the waist, his face toward the floor, his chest heaving. Drool spilled over his now-numb lips and hung in mid-air, slowly inching toward the ground, as viscous and yellow as honey.

Wally wiped his mouth with the back of his hand and tipped back the bottle yet again, this time, opening his mouth wide, letting the burning sensation hit the back of his throat, stunning and numbing him as he swallowed a gigantic gulp.

He could feel the liquid coming back up but Wally forced it back down again, a mighty croak emanating from deep within his chest. He exhaled, trying to control his breathing, readying himself for another swig. The second gulp went down much easier than the first, warming his innards. He took another gulp and another. Ten gulps in all as the bottle eventually emptied, only a thin coating of brown liquid clinging to the bottle's sides and bottom.

Wally was drunk, and he liked that he was numb. Finally, perhaps the memory of the past week would disappear like it never happened and life would go on, empty and alone but livable.

Booze made the dreams go away, the ones where Wally died or became maimed. He no longer feared he was going to die. Instead he was invincible, fortified by cloudy thinking, grogginess and inhibition. But the feeling eventually wore off. It always did, and Wally was transformed back into the scared, pathetic mope he'd become since Julie's death.

Wally released a boozey burp, the kind of stomach gas that could peel wallpaper. He covered his mouth and giggled, imagining Julie teasingly holding her nose as she wafted the foul odor away from her face. She mocked disgust, but Wally knew a smile would be hidden under her facade. Her bangs hung low, almost touching her dark eyebrows, teasing him as he yearned to brush them out of the way and plant a kiss on her forehead. Suddenly, she pointed at the bottle of brandy and shook her head disappointedly, frowning at the way he was dealing with his grief.

"Well--" Wally waved the bottle at the apparition as he slurred. "You have no say. You left me. Fuck you." He slammed the glass down on the table, slumped forward and buried his face in his arms, shame filling the hole in his heart. He sat up. "No. I take that back. Sorry."

Suddenly his stomach churned, and his mouth began to water. He rose to his feet as he spit into the now-empty bottle, steadying himself on the back of the chair as he stood. He took a few steps toward the bathroom but knew he wouldn't make it, stumbling as he reached his hands out like Frankenstein looking for his bride. The taste of his vomit was acrid, and his bile smelled like death. It splattered across the beautiful hardwood floors of the hallway, just two steps from the bathroom. It was thin and clear--he'd been drinking on an empty stomach--and spread outward, away from his slouched figure. Wally fell to his knees, thankfully short of the splatter and rested his head on the cool floor, positioned perfectly so he was eye level with Joey who was sitting in the doorway, head up, ears perked, seemingly on high alert.

"Hey, boy," Wally said as he reached over to scratch the dog's head. "I'm a mess, aren't I?"

Joey, accustomed to Wally's self-loathing over the past week, set his head down on the floor, and breathed out. The breeze hit Wally in the face, cooling his rapidly flushed cheeks and sweaty forehead.

"I was never much of a drinker," Wally whispered, closing his eyes. "I can't even mourn right." With his free hand, he wiped the bile from his mouth and tucked his arm under his body.

His mind beginning to wander and go into some dark territory, Wally turned over on his back, lying length wise down the hallway, his head near the bathroom and his feet by the living room. Joey continued to sit quietly, breathing softly, allowing Wally to rub the soft spot on top of his head between his ears. That's when the apartment started to spin.

The foghorn on the Golden Gate Bridge let out a low wail, signifying that the fog was rolling into the bay. Wally imagined the shadow streaming through the narrow channel, creeping toward the inner harbor where tourists walked the piers in Hawaiian shirts and khaki shorts, wolfing clam chowder in a sourdough bowl, laughing with each other, teasing the sea lions. Soon, it'd grow chilly, and they'd be shrouded in mist.

Suddenly, Wally found himself back to the day of Julie's

accident. He remembered being worried that Julie hadn't come home that Saturday morning. Their conversation while lying in bed, dreaming of their future together, seemed silly now, their optimistic view of life, of familyhood, their naive thinking that everything would be fine and that it was safe to bring a child into this cruel, cold world. He had tempted fate and the world had made him suffer for it quickly and judiciously, taking his wife moments after they had made their choice to finally start a family.

He remembered the call from a neighbor who had seen Joey standing guard and growling over Julie's body. The neighbor finally lured the dog away and a passerby administered first aid until a group of firefighters arrived on foot from just a block away. According to the neighbor, Julie had been careless, like she was wont to do, not watching where she was going, assuming that the approaching car would obey the stop sign and come to a halt. It hadn't. The driver was distracted. A cell phone? The radio? A screaming child? The bright sunny morning? It didn't matter. The driver plowed into the intersection, narrowly missing Joey but clipping Julie as she crossed, flinging her up in the air before depositing her a dozen feet away on the cold pavement.

Wally arrived at the hospital that day just as the EMTs were wheeling Julie into the emergency room. He could see that she was conscious but scared as their eyes met for a brief moment. A blood-soaked bandage was crusted against her forehead, sitting there between her hairline and eyebrows, looking like just another tie-dyed accessory to her outfit. A heavy-set nurse with big translucent goggles put her arm in front of Wally as he tried to enter the operation room, blocking his way. Let the doctors do their thing, she said, and

Wally was too confused to argue. It was over less than an hour later--the doctor coming out to the waiting room to give Wally the news as their friends looked on in horror.

Family members, including Julie's parents Bonnie and Nate came and went for the next several days, armed with sympathetic eyes and casseroles. Wally relented when Potey and Geoff insisted they make the funeral arrangements, taking away the responsibility he was so unprepared to take on. It didn't matter. Wally couldn't remember anything from the service. He assumed he got up to speak, but what he or anyone else had said was a mystery. Julie was buried in Daly City in a modest grave, a small marble headstone and a drumstick and a guitar pick to mark the location of her final resting place.

Then, life went on. The various aunts and uncles, cousins, they all called less often and came over even less. The casseroles ran out, and work wanted a timeline for when he would be coming back to the office. People simply acted as if nothing had happened. As if there wasn't a gigantic hole in Wally's heart. Nate and Bonnie continued to reach out, inviting him over for dinner that first week, but Wally wasn't ready to face them on his own, to make small talk with the only people who were in as much pain as he. Every time they'd call he'd let it go to voicemail--fearful, scared, unwilling to share in his grief.

Wally had never mourned before--his parents and all four of his grandparents were still alive--and his wife's was the first funeral he'd ever attended. As friends and family drifted away he wondered what he was supposed to do next. That's when he started to empty the liquor cabinet. Two types of rum. Vodka. A craft bottle of infused gin that Julie had brought back from a gig in Portland.

Wasn't this how people are supposed to grieve loved ones? he'd thought, pushing aside the empty bottles and finding the brandy a few moments before. I don't feel like I want to continue to drink, but isn't that what I'm supposed to do: fall into a drunken stupor?

But Wally had failed at that. What kind of drunk was he if he couldn't even hold down the liquor? He hadn't felt the effects--the carelessness, the numbness, the detached feelings--for more than a few seconds before his body rejected the brandy, splattering it all over the hardwood floors, a metaphor for his shattered state.

6

He was old. An old man with a long white beard. He's sitting at a modest kitchen table, a bowl of soggy cereal and a glass of juice in front of him. His eyes are downcast, pulled down under droopy eyelids covered in cysts and ingrown hairs. His hands shake as he lifts the spoon to his mouth. He gets halfway up and the air goes out of his lungs. There's no use. He sets the spoon aside, pushes the bowl in front of him and lays his head down on the table, forehead down, his nose smushed against the table top. He closes his eyes. There's no use going on. He's alone and sad and tired, and he's ready to die.

It's well past midnight, and the apartment is dark save for the light emanating from the TV in the corner. Wally sits upright on the floor, his duvet wrapped around his body and pushed up over his head. Joey is in his lap, his neck craned so that his head is poking out of the blanket just below Wally's chin. The two peer out of their cave up at the TV in front of them,

Wally's face in shadow except the end of his pointy nose and tear-streaked cheeks. He's watching a younger, happier, healthier version of himself dressed in a tailored tuxedo sitting at a small round table set for two. Wally is pale in the video, his red lips bursting from his white complexion.

Wally remembered that Julie had convinced him--actually tricked him--into getting his eyebrows trimmed that morning at a day spa in the Sacramento River Valley. Just twenty-four years old, he'd never been to a spa in his life and guffawed when Julie suggested he get sculpted.

"This is our wedding," she implored. "If there's any day to do this, it's today."

Wally continued to protest, but Julie calmly picked up the phone and made the appointment for him. An hour later, he was laying on his back on a massage bench, staring at the ceiling, a terrycloth robe hugging his otherwise naked body. He remembered the acute pain as each hair was ripped off his brow, the split-second of panic and then the calming attendant putting pressure on the spot previously sporting the vacated follicle. This went on for fifteen minutes as Wally suffered through a range of emotions from panic to euphoria to calm and back to panic. Needless to say it wasn't the healthiest morning activity on his wedding day.

Next to sleek-browed Wally in the video, Julie looks gorgeous in her white satin wedding dress, a crown of flowers ringed around her head, her hair down, big loopy curls set gently on her shoulders. Of Italian heritage, she's tan and calm and confident. She turns to the younger Wally and smiles, unmistakably happy. The camera zooms in and Wally sees the moment he knew he'd made the right decision to marry this wonderful woman, the instant she made him feel like a man worthy of her company. Under the tablecloth, you can see Julie reach out and put her hand on Wally's thigh, gently stroking it before giving him a little squeeze. A simple gesture, the act filled him with confidence and gave him the strength to make it through the reception. She has chosen me, so I must be special, Wally remembered thinking that afternoon, the most important of his life, the day he understood what it meant to share his life with someone and have someone share her life with him.

Now alone--save for Joey--in his dark apartment Wally lowered his head and wept, his heart aching for Julie to reach out and again touch his thigh under the table, to give him that feeling of invincibility again, to make him feel chosen.

On screen, the camera pans left to center stage where Wally's college roommate takes the microphone.

"Uh, hi there. I'm Sebastian, Wally's best man, and, uh, I guess it's time for me to give my toast." He's wearing a tux similar to Wally's, but the top button of his shirt is undone and the bowtie is unclasped and hanging off to the side. He has a tumbler of rye in one hand and grasps the microphone stand with his other. He looks loose and indifferent like he is in one of those old fashioned cigarette commercials, smooth, a rebel without a cause.

"I had the pleasure of being one of the first of Wally's college buddies to meet Julie," he begins. "Julie? Jules? Isn't that what you call her?" Sebastian gestures off camera with his drink hand, his index finger extended from his glass as he points.

"Anyway, I came to San Francisco for some business and

Wally invited me out with this musician he was dating. Honestly, I didn't know what to expect. Purple hair? Mohawk? Ripped jean jacket?" He pauses while the crowd hoots, flashing a mischievous smile. "Anyway-- we had a great night. Julie turned out to be nice and seemed to really like Wally, and Wally seemed relaxed--though that could have been the eight or nine Amstel Lights he put down that night. On the walk back up to Wally's apartment, I braced for the inevitable. As we all know, Wally can be a little nervous or anxious around women. Especially when he first starts dating someone--which isn't too often. It's not that Wally analyzes every detail. It's that he OVER-analyzes every detail."

There are some guffaws from the crowd, and Sebastian pushes on. "So knowing that we'd be chugging up this steep hill in San Francisco for about fifteen minutes, I braced myself for a long marathon of neurotic analysis. 'Sebastian, do you think she likes me?' 'She's smart, right?' 'Do you think she noticed when I spilled beer on the bartender?' 'She drinks scotch and sodas. What does that mean?' Needless to say, I was prepared for the worst."

At this point, Sebastian shuffles his stance, correcting his posture, standing straight in front of the mic. "But to my surprise, instead of questioning every detail, Wally started speaking in declarative sentences. 'She's intelligent and pretty.' 'I like talking to her.' 'She makes me smile.' 'She's a cool chick.' I was completely floored. He was calm, collected, confident even. No analysis. No second guessing. I thought about what he was saying and how he was saying it. I thought about the great time we had, and how understanding and patient Julie had been. I thought that maybe, just maybe, she is different. Maybe she is the one. And maybe one day, if I was so lucky and so honored, I'd be up here giving this toast tonight. So Jules--" Sebastian raises his glass and looks off-camera. "I just want to say that for once Wally is right. You are beautiful. You are intelligent. You are a pretty cool chick. And we are all happy that Wally found his better half. Let's raise our glass. Good luck, and best wishes to the happy couple. Congratulations. Cheers!"

As the camera pans back to the two newlyweds at their table the crowd cheers lustily and toasts the couple. Wally, a wide grin across his face, leans over and passionately kisses Julie. His kiss is long and deep, and Julie looks a bit surprised at first but then visibly relaxes in his arms, succumbing to his passion. The crowd audibly hoots in the background as the camera zooms in showing Wally's hand reaching out and gently stroking Julie's thigh.

In the apartment Wally broke down. Tears streaming down his face, he bowed his head, nuzzling the top of Joey's soft head. The dog turned his head and sniffed Wally's neck and his tongue flicked out, wetting his master's skin. Wally pulled Joey in closer, hugging him tightly, wrapping his arms around his warm body. Wally could feel Joey breathing--in and out, in and out--and matched his rhythm--the two of them heaving in unison.

"I'm never going to have that again," Wally sobbed in Joey's ear.

The dog continued to nuzzle Wally's neck, his soft fur tickling Wally's skin. Wally sighed and pulled his head back.

The dog craned his neck so he was looking up at Wally who cupped Joey's face and brought it to his own.

"You'll do just fine, Joey," he said, rubbing his hot nose against Joey's snout. "You'll do just fine."

7

Wally pulled the collar of his shirt up around his neck, bracing against the frigid wind. He was high now, up on a ridge in the Presidio overlooking Chrissy Field Beach where they'd collected the rocks for Julie's hypothetical garden. It would never be tilled, Wally thought as he neared a small trail that led to the bridge. The idea of their garden was dead just like his wife.

He climbed the orange stairway just as the sun went down on the other side of the Golden Gate, the fiery globe melting into the Pacific Ocean between land that jutted out from Marin County to the North and Lands End to the South. The fog was rolling in as well, one of those picturesque evenings when the light bounced off the Golden Gate Bridge as the orange structure disappeared in the haze. The steel beams looked like they were on fire, the gateway to the end of the earth, an opening to hell.

Wally kept going, his hands shoved in his pockets, head scrunched down, eyes focused ahead. He passed the 1950s-style visitor center and went out on the walkway that crossed the bridge. Six lanes of traffic streamed past on his left; a chasm opened up on his right. The first hundred feet or so would be above the cliff that guards the harbor, but soon he'd be over freezing water. The fog was streaming over the span now, the air current taking it up and over the roadway, through the steel supports, over Wally's head and down over the railing on the other side. There, it cascaded down, like roiling rapids until it eventually returned to the airstream a few meters above the water.

Tourists were heading in the opposite direction toward the visitor center and the city, most wearing shorts and T-shirts, unprepared for the typical 20-degree cool off when the sun went down and the fog seeped back into the bay. They were huddled like Wally who still strode with his hands jammed in his pockets, but while Wally had a determined look on his face, the tourists wore expressions of amusement.

When Wally was about a quarter of the way across the bridge he was alone. The fog kept his visibility to twenty feet in either direction but the sound carried further in the heavy air. He stopped and faced east, his back to traffic overlooking what should have been the island of Alcatraz in the distance if it hadn't been obscured. He spread his arms and placed his palms on the railing. He leaned forward and looked down. The choppy water was barely visible through the mist but he knew it was there. It had to be there.

Wally took off his jacket and draped it over the railing. Stepping back, he took a deep, determined breath and closed his eyes. He said a short prayer, something about being thankful that he would soon have peace and made a motion to swing his leg up on the rail.

"Hey there, friend," came a voice. Wally paused, turned

to his right and saw a silhouette of a figure through the fog. The wind wisped the clouds around him as the speaker took a step forward and came into focus.

"Fuck," Wally muttered. It was a cop. The man's tan State Highway Patrol uniform cut an imposing figure, and his silver star on his chest reflected the only light that was able to get through the fog.

"What's your name?" asked the man.

Wally was still frozen with one leg straddling the railing. One swift movement and he would be over.

"I'm Wally."

The man nodded.

"Hi, Wally. I'm Stan."

"I'm going to jump."

"I figured that when I saw your determined face walk past the visitors' center. I'm here to make sure you don't."

Wally paused.

"Why do you care?"

"It's my job to care."

Wally thought about this.

"So you don't really care, do you?"

The man took another step forward.

"Of course I do."

"I'm going to do it."

"I know you are, Wally. But can we have a conversation first?"

"What for?"

"Paperwork. You jump, and I have a lot of paperwork to fill out. It would be cool if you'd help me out with some of the details."

Wally smiled. I'll play along, he thought.

"Ok. What do you want to know?"
"Your name. Wally--?"
"Drummond."
"Wally Drummond. Ok. Address?"
"Seventeen-forty-eight Polk Street."
"Polk Gulch neighborhood?"
"Yeah."
"Next of kin."
"None."
"Interesting."
Wally paused. "What do you mean?"
"Oh, nothing. It's just that it doesn't seem like a young single man from Polk Gulch would have much to be depressed about?"
"You don't know me."
"No. No. I suppose not. Anything in your pockets?"
"My pockets? Why?"

Stan took another step forward but Wally guessed that he was still about twelve feet away, well outside lunging distance.

"Standard procedure. You know, we can't have rescue personnel stuck with needles when they haul you out. You know, AIDS and all."
"No. Nothing in my pockets."
"What about your wallet? Phone, keys, things like that. They aren't in your pockets?"
"Everything's in my jacket."

Wally gestured at his jacket on the railing.
"This is your coat?"
"Yeah."
"Can I have it?"

"What?"

"You're not going to need it anymore."

Wally shrugged. He picked up the jacket and tossed it gently at the officer's feet. "Put it to good use," he said.

"Right. Because you don't need it where you're going."

"That's right."

Stan picked up the jacket, wrapped it in a ball and tossed the bundle behind him down the walkway.

"What's your next question?" Wally asked.

"Why would be a good start."

"My wife died."

"And you were close?"

"She was my wife." Wally instinctively reached for his wedding ring, twisting the cold medal around his finger.

"Tell me about the ring."

"It's my wedding ring."

"Toss it over here, and I'll make sure it gets to whoever you want."

"I want to take it with me."

"I see. So you think that by killing yourself you'll be able to see your wife again?"

"I'm tired."

"Ah. So this is about you, not her."

"You can look at it that way."

"Ok. So, no kids. Any family members we can contact?"

"No."

"Friends?"

"They were really all my wife's friends."

"I see. You're one of those loner types. Anyone at all in your life?"

"Just a dog. He'll get over it."

Stan nodded.

"Ok, great talking to you," Wally continued. "In I go." He swung the rest of his body over the rail so that now he was facing the sidewalk and traffic with the cold drop behind him.

"No wait. We're not done here," Stan shouted. Wally paused, thinking that the cop sounded angry, not compassionate like he would have thought. "I still have some questions for you. This isn't some simple one-page form we're talking about here. A suicide is a pretty big thing. Traffic backs up. Tourists get upset. Questions need to be answered. Did you know that they want to put up a net? What do you think about that?"

Wally shook his head. "Right now, I'm not in favor."

Stan chuckled. "No, I guess you're right. You wouldn't be."

Wally nodded. His patience was running thin.

"Tell me what you did today, Wally. I want to get a sense of your last couple of hours. You know, for the eulogy."

"Nothing much. I was just watching my old wedding video with my dog."

"Oh, no. Not the wedding video. Rookie move."

"Rookie move?"

"Yeah, never watch your wedding video. Way too many memories there. At least not for a few years. How long ago did she pass?"

"Three weeks."

Stan whistled. "Ouch. Still a fresh wound, then."

"Listen, I'm done talking. I'm tired. I want this to end."

"There are people who can help, you know."

"I'm already on anti-depressants."

"Pills alone aren't the answer. We can get you to talk to someone."

"Not interested."

"Ok. I had to try. The form makes me at least try. Ok. Just a few more questions and then I'll let you--"

Stan mimed a jumping motion by cupping his hand and clawing at the air, dropping his hand below his waist.

"Tell me what you're going to do tomorrow," he continued.

Wally looked up. "What do you mean? I'm not doing anything tomorrow."

"Right, right. Well what did you have planned before you were going to jump?"

"Work, I guess."

"Where do you work?"

"A software company. I'm in sales."

"Sounds awful."

"What?"

"I mean, I couldn't do it. Chained to a desk all day. Staring at a computer. I need to be outside. Walking the beat. I would do anything to avoid paperwork."

"Hence our little conversation here."

"That's right, Wally. By giving me all this information you're helping me avoid making a bunch of phone calls and staying inside all day tomorrow."

"Glad I can help."

"So, in all seriousness," Stan continued, "You really think your dog--what's his name?--"

"Joey."

"You really think Joey will be all right? I mean, who's going to feed him? Or walk him?"

"Someone will adopt him, and he'll forget about me in a week."

"I don't know. Sometimes these dogs that go through trauma are really broken."

"What do you mean?"

"Well presumably this dog is just as broken up about your wife's passing as you are. And now you want to take away the one person he has left? Poor dog."

"I guess. He'll be fine, though. He's a whore. He'll cuddle up to anyone willing to scratch behind his ears."

Stan chuckled. "Yeah, dogs are like that, aren't they? But cuddling up to a stranger is different than full-on, unconditional love. Contrary to belief, dogs do grieve and can't just move on."

Wally thought back to his apartment when he and Joey watched the wedding video--feeling the dog's warm body against his, his soft fur, the comforting lick. Had Joey been reassuring him?

"To be honest with you, he'll probably be destroyed," Stan continued.

Wally flinched at the word destroyed. It was harsh, unemotional, indifferent.

"Seriously, I've seen it before. The dog gets depressed, confused, lashes out at anyone and anything. It could have been the most happy-go-lucky creature in the world before, but then something just snaps. Like the grief changes their brain chemistry. Maybe he'll get lucky, and one of these rescue groups takes him in. But then he'll be crammed into some foster home with half a dozen other dogs. Maybe he'll get better. But not likely."

Wally then thought back to the day Julie died. The

reports from neighbors and witnesses that Joey stood guard over Julie's body, not letting anyone near. In the days after, seemingly moping around the apartment, the disappearance of that never-ending Jack Russel well of energy. Refusing to go near the intersection where the accident happened. Wally looked up at Stan who was still standing a dozen feet or so away, knees locked, hands behind his back, not exactly on alert if Wally decided to make a move off the edge of the bridge. All he had to do now was to let go, open his hands, stretch out his fingers and--fall.

"Let me buy you a cup of coffee, Mr. Drummond," Stan said, stretching out his arms. "It's time to come back over that rail and take care of that dog."

Wally lowered his head, let out a long exhale and tossed his leg back over the railing. He swung the rest of his body over the metal bar and dropped to the pavement, two feet firmly planted on the pedestrian walkway.

"I'd like that," Wally stammered and grabbed Stan in an embrace. The two men held each other as the wind and fog swirled up and over the bridge. Wally grasped Stan's tan uniform tightly in his fists and buried his face in the large man's chest, sobbing uncontrollably.

"Let's give your wife's friends a call," Stan said.

8

Wally felt no pain, but he knew he was finished. He could feel the mugger's cold blade inside his gut. He looked up into the man's face, making eye contact, seeing nothing but fear and uncertainty. Wally clutched at his attacker's body; it was all bones and sinew, and there was crust around the man's mouth. An addict. Wally recognized the desperation. A wave of sorrow washed over him, recognizing his death would haunt this young man for the rest of his life--if he ever got sober. Wally tried to mouth a few encouraging words but they were drowned out by the blood bubbling up his throat. He collapsed face down against the sidewalk, one eye ripped open from the force. The other one, the good eye, started to fade out as a pair of ragged penny loafers retreated down the dark street.

The sun beat down, warming Wally's face, making him feel flushed. He hungrily looked down at the arugula and walnut salad set in front of him, his stomach eliciting a low rumble as he waited for Abby to join him at the sidewalk table. He craned his neck and peered through the large plate glass window into the cafe, eagerly wondering when her turkey sandwich would finally appear on the counter. His salad was ready five minutes ago, and he'd told her he'd wait for her before digging in.

Wally reached down and stroked Joey's soft fur between his ears. The dog was lying on the sidewalk under the table, his tongue wagging, a water bowl at his feet. Wally silently cursed himself for skipping breakfast this morning. A glass of orange juice and an anti-depressant were the only things he'd consumed today, and it was already early afternoon.

It had been a few weeks since Wally climbed back over the railing and allowed Stan the Highway Patrolman to buy him a cup of coffee. In the days after, Wally called Abby and told her everything. She didn't say much but kept checking in on Wally, taking him out to lunch or a hike or making sure he had fresh groceries in his apartment. Sometimes they'd just drive for hours on backcountry roads in hilly Marin, Abby's iPhone playlist on Nineties grunge. She literally kept him alive. Not in the medical sense or even emotionally. She made sure the day-to-day things--like eating and interacting with the rest of the world--got done.

Wally's phone had buzzed at eight that morning with a text invitation to lunch. It had kept buzzing every hour until he finally surrendered and met Abby at Nook, a cafe and wine bar on Nob Hill a few blocks from his building. As he'd got ready to walk out the door, he'd decided to bring Joey who looked more than happy to get some exercise and fresh air.

Wally peered into the cafe again, seeing Abby leaning against the far wall, staring intently at her smartphone, sweeping her finger up and down and side to side along the screen. She was dressed casually, wearing a blue, ribbed tank top and jeans. Her red hair was tied back in a messy ponytail that brushed across her shoulder blades as she looked up from her phone to see if her sandwich had appeared on the counter in front of her.

Wally frowned as a cable car loaded with tourists hanging out the side rumbled past and turned onto Hyde Street from Washington. An older woman, a shopping bag secured around her elbow, pointed to Joey, her mouth exclaiming as they passed. Her fellow passengers, including an elderly man who was presumably her husband, smiled, their eyes lighting up at the sight of a cute, cuddly dog lying under a restaurant table. Screeching metal on metal echoed across the intersection as the brakeman slingshot the car around the corner, transferring from the east-west underground cable to the north-south line in a single swift movement. The conductor rattled out on the car's bell a nursery rhyme that Wally couldn't quite place--ding, ding, duh-ding, ding, ding--as the car swung out into traffic and headed down into the valley between Nob and Russian Hills.

Finally, Abby emerged from the front door, and smiling, slid her sunglasses down over her eyes as she put her plate down on the table. She bent to give Joey a good rub on top of his head before she sat. As soon as her butt hit the seat, Wally stabbed at his pile of greens and stuffed a forkful in his mouth.

"Hungry much," Abby teased as she scooted in.

Wally responded by taking another mouthful.

"Well, I see your mourning hasn't affected your appetite."

Wally stopped in mid chew and frowned, narrowing his eyes for better affect.

"Sorry." Abby sighed. "That was rude."

Wally shrugged and continued to munch on his salad. They sat in silence, Wally stuffing his face with arugula while Abby took a few careful bites of her sandwich, her bare shoulders glistening, pale skin starting to turn pink.

"So, how are you doing, Wally?"

Wally shrugged again.

"You have enough food at your place? You out of coffee? Dog food?"

Wally shrugged for the third time. Abby smiled, reaching across the table to touch Wally's arm, but he instinctively pulled back and, catching himself tried to play it off by picking up his fork.

"How's Joey?" Abby continued.

"He's fine. Though I slept in a little late this morning. His tail was curled down between his legs around his penis, squeezing it tight."

"See, a joke. That's good."

Wally made a face and, fork in hand, returned to his now half-eaten salad. Joey continued to sit under the table, oblivious they were talking about him, happy to be outside where he could soak up the sunshine. He hadn't been out much in the two months since Julie's death other than his morning and afternoon walks with Wally. And those were usually pretty short, more business than pleasure.

Abby picked up her sandwich, nibbling the corner here and there, but hardly eating much. Instead, she focused on Wally, watching him shovel green leaves, walnuts and blue cheese in his mouth, dressing coating his lips, making them slippery, oily. Wally suddenly became self-conscious, remembering he hadn't showered that morning and his hair was unwashed and due for a trim. He wiped his mouth with the back of his hand and licked his lips and then the side of his mouth. A hint of mint toothpaste mixed with the vinegary dressing.

"You know, we're all worried about you," Abby said. "Annette, Xander, Julie's parents. Potey said he wants to take you out soon--"

Wally dropped his fork onto his plate and looked up.

"Listen," he said. "What I told you wasn't necessarily in confidence, but I don't like the thought of all you guys talking about me."

Abby continued. "I'm sorry, but we really are all worried about you."

Wally paused, fork in midair piled with arugula, half-way to his mouth. He broke eye contact with Abby and looked up, past the tree branches towering over the intersection, at the light-blue sky.

"It was just a momentary slip," Wally whispered. "I don't want to hurt myself anymore. I don't."

"I know. I know."

This time Wally allowed her to place her hand gingerly on his arm. "I can't help thinking that it should have been me," he said. "I was sure it was going to be me."

"Hey, hey, I know. I know." Abby rubbed her fingers up and down Wally's arm, the static electricity sending the ends of his hair there up on end.

Wally looked at his plate and set down the fork, surprised about the confession that had come out of his mouth. It was pure guilt and regret, spoken aloud for the first time. He took a few gulps of water then continued eating. Abby just sat there, staring at him, and her face softened.

"Listen, Wally," she said, continuing to rub his arm in comfort. "I know. We all know. You have every right in the world to feel guilty or foolish or whatever emotion you want to feel right now. Your wife just died. No one expects anything out of you right now except grief and confusion. We're here to help--that's all. We want to help you deal with this however you want, in your own way, without any interference or judgement or misunderstandings at all. The only thing we ask is that you don't try to hurt yourself again."

Wally pulled out of Abby's grasp and buried his face in his hands. He rubbed his eyes and his temples, trying to calm himself.

Finally Abby spoke again, "Is that your wedding ring?"

Wally lifted his face out of his hands, and red, blurry eyes, turned his left hand over, and glanced at the heavy platinum band on his finger.

"Yeah, I guess it is." He really hadn't thought about it since Julie's death. It had been a part of him for a long time, almost part of his body. "So?"

"You're still wearing it." Wally was relieved that she said it as a statement rather than a question. He nodded.

"I think that's sweet."

The sun had warmed up the grey hoodie Wally was wearing, and he was starting to sweat. He could feel moisture collecting under his arms and a trickle starting to run down his side. He reached into his pocket and pulled out a pair of aviator sunglasses and placed them on his face, shielding his moist eyes. Abby watched him from across the table, her lips curled into a slight, loving smile.

Wally relaxed his posture and continued eating. They sat in silence again for a few moments. Wally stared intently at his salad while Abby looked around at the sidewalk scape, the other tables and customers, the planters, the cable car stop up the street, the passing traffic. She absentmindedly redid her ponytail as she looked around.

"Here. Give me your ring." She up-turned her hand so that the tips of her fingers could grasp the band. Wally flinched, taken aback by the request, but recovered and drew his hands together. He struggled to free the platinum ring from his finger, but it eventually slipped off. It felt heavy in his hand, much heavier than he remembered. He turned it over, rubbing the inlay, feeling the textured etching with the tips of his fingers. On the inside, he could barely make out the inscription that Julie had commissioned and wouldn't let him see until their wedding night. It was a quote from her favorite movie, Little Women: "Forgive Each Other. Begin Again Tomorrow."

Wally plopped the ring in Abby's outstretched hand, his own hand lingering for a second before she pulled away. Abby put the ring on the table in front of her and reached behind her neck, unclasping a thin white gold chain. She brought it around and looped it through Wally's ring, picking up the two ends so the band hung loosely above the table between them.

"Here." Abby reached out as Wally leaned forward. She clasped the chain behind his neck, and the ring fell to his chest with a thump, warm and heavy against his hoodie. He tucked it under his shirt and it lay against his chest, itching the skin where it touched.

Abby smiled.

"How's the paperwork coming along--you know, Julie's bills, social security, things like that?" she asked.

"Everything's a lot tougher than I thought," Wally responded. "Everyone wants to see a death certificate. The bank, PG&E, the credit card companies. I've started carrying it around with me. As you know, all the bills were in her name. Everything."

Abby smiled. "Just think. You loved her so much you wanted to shield her from doing all that in case you passed. You are such a sweet husband. Julie really adored you. She loved you."

Wally knew it was true. They were married, so of course Julie loved him. But deep down, he'd always had his doubts about how a woman as wonderful as Julie could love someone like him. He fell in love with her that night in Vertigo when she was on stage, and he knew he'd gotten lucky when she eventually let him take her out on a date. After that he simply refused to let her go. He knew that eventually he would wear her down and they would end up together. And that's exactly what had happened.

Wally looked up at Abby. "You can't prepare someone for something like this," he said, looking earnestly into her eyes while fingering his ring under his shirt. "You just can't. It's impossible. I shouldn't have even tried."

Abby reached across the table, taking Wally's hand in hers. She gave it a slight squeeze, showing him that she understood.

"Can you imagine if you tried to go out on a date, like you told her to do?" she said.

"Oh God, no way. Not even close to being able to go out. I was a moron to suggest that Julie move on quickly. Now that I'm going through it, I just don't--I don't--I don't--what was I was thinking?"

"You'll know when the time is right. You won't plan it. You won't think about it. It'll just happen."

Wally shrugged. "Maybe. That's just not on my radar."

"Of course. But when it is, let me know."

"What? Why?"

"So we can talk about it. Please, just do it."

Wally nodded, and Abby smiled.

"In the meantime, get out of the house. Give Xander a call. He always liked you. And, I can't believe I'm about to suggest this, but go out with Potey. It would be good for you."

Wally silently shook his head, leaned back in his chair and raised his chin to the sky, letting the sun fall on his face. It was warm, and Wally was surprised that it made him feel good. He could hear some birds chirping from a big magnolia tree on the corner. Wind rustled through the leaves. There was a faint clanking sound as another cable car approached from behind. It felt like spring.

Suddenly, just as quickly as the warm washed over Wally, it disappeared. A cloud moved over the sun and the air grew chilly, cold even. Joey barked from under the table, and Wally sat upright. Abby shuddered from the cool breeze as a car horn sounded, scattering the birds. And, then, right there, Wally realized that the pain would likely never go away. There might be moments of warmth and calmness, but the cold would always creep back.

9

Wally sat at a long oaken dining room table, sitting straight up, his back against a solid straight-back chair, his hands folded and in his lap. The room was white, painfully white. The kind of brightness that made you squint your eyes to avoid blindness. Footsteps echoed off a far-away wall, growing louder as someone approached. A sort of tap, tap, tap. Abby appeared, wearing a formal serving suit: black coat and pants, white shirt, white gloves. She was carrying a metal tray, covered by one of those rounded metal lids. She approached the table, circled to Wally's right and placed the tray in front of him. She pulled off the lid with a flourish revealing an appetizing-looking omelet on a white plate. A sprig of garnish sat off to the side.

Abby retreated, and Wally looked hungrily at the food. Picking up a fork, he poked the omelet, and a blob of gooey cheddar cheese oozed out. He cut off a bite, equal parts egg, cheese and mushroom, and popped it into his mouth. An explosion of flavor spread throughout his mouth--on his tongue, the back of his throat--even his teeth could taste the morsels. He swallowed and took another bite. Then another. And another.

The omelet was half gone when Wally noticed he was sweating--a lot. He loosened his collar and pushed back from the table. His sinus cavities started to get stuffed up, and he could feel his throat swell. The room began to spin around him. The table ended up on the ceiling, then on the floor and back again. Wally fell to his knees, gasping for breath. Abby now stood over him, arms to her side, a sweet smile plastered on her face. She held up a bag of soil-crusted fungi that looked like they'd just been picked. Were they the edible kind? Blood streaked tears ran down Abby's face as Wally fell face-first on the floor.

A loud buzzer sounded, and Joey went ape shit. Barking incessantly while chasing his tail around in circles, the dog was supremely over-stimulated, ears pinned back, teeth bared, eyes glazed over. Just a few moments before, he was curled up on the living room rug, passed out, dead to the world. The buzzer had sent him from zero to sixty in nothing flat.

Wally was a different story. The buzzer had woken him up from a nap as well, but he remained on the couch, blanket pulled up to his chin, unaffected as Joey ran rampant around the apartment. The buzzer went off again, and Wally slowly swung his legs around, planted them firmly on the floor and sat up. He took his time stretching, rubbing the sleep out of his eyes, prepping his body for the ten-foot walk to the intercom. He put one foot in front of the other as Joey continued to run in circles, yipping from excitement.

"Hello?" Wally mumbled into the speaker.

"Walt the Gestalt, it's Potey. Let me up."

Wally hesitated before finally pressing the door unlock button and made his way back to the couch. Wally could hear the heavy footsteps coming up the stairs. Potey was anything but subtle, bounding into the room, waving his arms like a crazy person, his normally slicked-back hair now wild and blazing. Joey jumped up and pushed off Potey's crotch with all four paws, propelling himself backward toward the living room. He twisted in mid-air, landing on his feet and continued to run in circles.

"Hey, buddy," exclaimed Potey as he pulled off his sport coat and hung it on a hook in the hallway. "How's my favorite pooch?"

He bent down and grabbed at Joey's tail, sending the dog into another crazed lap around the room. Wally swung his legs back up on the couch and lay back.

"No. Absolutely not," Potey said when he saw Wally. "It's Friday night. I'm taking you out."

Wally closed his eyes. "I've had a long week at work. I think it's a Netflix night."

Potey stepped into the living room. He was wearing a yellow button-down shirt, black slacks and dress shoes. Wally figured he stopped by on his way from his home office in Laurel Heights to some happy hour location downtown. His eyes were afire and his cheeks were flushed. Wally couldn't be sure if his condition was from walking up the stairs or if he'd already started the weekend on his own.

"When was the last time you left the apartment?" Potey

asked, hands on hips.

"I, uh--"

"Not counting taking the dog out."

"This morning. For work."

Potey shook his head.

"When was the last time you left the apartment to do something fun?"

"I had lunch with Abby last weekend--"

"Nope. That's sad. We're going out. Where are your shoes?" Potey looked behind him at the floor near the front door, spotting Wally's sneakers lying under the coat rack, next to an umbrella stand.

"Seriously, Potey. I appreciate it, but I'm staying in tonight."

"Shit, man. You are one depressed mother fucker. It's not healthy for you to stay in. Come on. I'm meeting some buddies from my tech PR days at Norton's Vault. First round's on me."

Wally didn't move.

"I'm not one of those people who have to go out on the weekend. It's ok to stay in some nights."

Potey snorted. "Yeah. They're called Tuesdays. We're going."

"We're not."

Wally heard Potey take a seat on an oversized recliner by the window and settle in. There were muffled sounds as Potey pushed back in the chair, activating the footrest that swung up, supporting his feet. They sat in silence for a few moments, Wally resting peacefully, eyes closed, on the couch, Potey with ants in his pants, unable to sit still, fidgeting in the chair. Joey had managed to maintain his excitement and was lying in the attack position on the rug, one of Wally's sneakers between his paws, a shoelace sticking out of his clenched jaw.

Wally opened his eyes to peek across the room at Potey. Something had caught Potey's attention on the windowsill, and he'd craned his neck to peer behind the curtains that framed the window.

"What's in that glass vase?" he asked, pointing to the collection of seashells and rocks that Wally and Julie had collected on the beach for their eventual garden. It was three quarters full, at least twenty percent fuller than when Julie had passed away.

"Nothing. It belonged to Jules."

Potey kept looking at the vase. Wally could see him wrinkling his nose, perturbed about something.

"What?"

Potey snapped out of his trance, shaking his head. He pushed the footrest back into the base of the recliner and stood up, sidestepping past the TV and in front of the window. He reached out and picked up the vase and took a step back.

"What do you think you're doing?" Wally exclaimed, feeling panic come bubbling up. "That's Julie's vase. I got those shells for her."

"Why're you holding onto it? I mean, it's not like she's going to need it back."

Potey paused for a split second, as if deciding something, then walked across the room toward the front door still holding the vase.

"Where are you taking that?"

"It's going down the garbage chute."

Wally jumped up off the couch in one quick motion, barring Potey from taking another step.

"Put it down."

Potey seemed surprised and hesitated, but just for a second as he moved toward the door. Wally sidestepped in front of him, blocking his way yet again. Wally raised his hand and wagged a finger in Potey's face. He was shaking, uncontrollably, from his fingers to his toes. His face grew hot, and he noticed Joey slowly pick himself up and slink out of the room.

"I don't want to upset you," Potey said as he held his ground. "But this is going. It'll be healthy for you."

"Will everyone quit telling me what's good for me?" Wally spoke slowly and softly, measured like he was making every word count.

"Did someone say something?"

"Abby. She said I need to get out more."

"I know. She called me after your lunch."

"She--and you--need to mind your own business."

"Sorry, bro. This is going to hurt." Potey took another step toward the door, but Wally swung his hip out to the side, checking Potey, sending him sprawling across the room. He lost hold of the vase as he went to the ground, batting it around like a fumbled football before a final swat sent it flying through the kitchen doorway. It hit the wall and miraculously bounced off, unbroken, and still in one piece. For a split second, as the vase hovered intact in the air, Wally felt a rush of relief. Perhaps it would be all right. Then, slow-motion over, the vase hit the linoleum floor and shattered in a thousand pieces, scattering glass, rocks and shells from the stove to the fridge.

"You bastard!"

Wally lunged and landed on top of Potey on the floor, desperately clawing at Potey's face and going for the bigger man's neck. Wally squeezed as hard as he could, trying to crush the life out of the stupid, inconsiderate man. Potey called out and was able to get his hand between Wally's hands and his throat.

Joey ran into the room, fiercely barking at Potey who by now had easily grabbed hold of Wally's arms and twisted them behind his back. He balanced himself with one hand on the floor and stood up, still holding onto Wally with his other hand. Potey swung Wally around so he was between him and Joey whose barking grew more aggressive as spittle flew out of his snout.

Wally continued to flail about, desperately trying to wriggle free and hurt Potey. He was facing Joey, and, as their eyes met, Wally felt a pang of helplessness and shame. An Alpha male had come into their home and easily over-matched him in front of his dog--an animal who didn't piss on the floor or chew on the baseboards for the single reason that Wally was the dominant member of the pack. And now, he'd been emasculated.

Doing what most over-matched fighters do when they have no other choice, Wally instinctively went dirty, kicking Potey full-force in the shin. Pain seared through Wally's unshod foot as both men fell to their knees. Wally clutched at his toes--were they broken?--momentarily losing track of Potey, who wasn't worse for the wear given that his attacker wasn't wearing any shoes.

Joey attached himself to Potey's ankle as the bigger man stood over Wally and picked him up by the armpits, tossing him on the couch. He then shook Joey off, picked up Wally's shoe and flung it across the room where it landed in Wally's splayed-out lap.

Instinctively, Wally curled up on his side into the fetal position and stayed there, unmoving. Suddenly, Potey was on him, sitting on the side of his body, crushing his ribs, forcing all the air out of Wally's lungs. Joey circled the coffee table in the middle of the room, barking incessantly as the two men wrestled on the couch. Wally squirmed but Potey had at least seventy-five pounds on him, and he was weak from months of inactivity. Potey was bouncing up and down on him now, and he could feel Potey's butt crack opening and closing around his hip. Hot and sticky air washed over them as they struggled.

"Are you farting on me? Ugh! Get the fuck off," Wally yelled, placing his hands against the back of the couch. He pushed with all his strength and managed to slide out from under Potey and crash to the floor. He dragged himself across the room on his elbows like they did in old Vietnam War movies, using his knees and wrists as leverage, as Joey nosed him in the ribs for encouragement.

"Enough," Potey said as he sat calmly on the couch, watching Wally crawl across the floor. His eyebrows were arched as if he were impressed. Wally stopped and flipped over on his back. Joey jumped up on his chest and started licking his face. Wally sat up and nuzzled the dog against his chest. Breathing hard, he stared up at Potey from his position on the floor.

"Strip club?" Potey asked hopefully, sensing a shift in the mood.

"Fine, Potey. You win. I'll get my shoes."

10

Four nipples stared at him from on stage, each more gruesome than the next. Despite the fact that they belonged to two women, no two areolas were the same, seeming having been deformed during some discount plastic surgery session. The buxom woman hanging upside down with her legs wrapped around a pole had one nipple pointed up and the other pointing down. Both were being shook in Wally's direction. Her equally endowed colleague was belly down, legs splayed out behind her, grinding her groin on the black-lacquered floor. A big spotlight shone behind her, reflecting off the spot right beneath her crotch. She was right at the edge of the stage hovering over Wally and Potey, her breasts hanging over their heads. Her nipples were both pointed out to the side, so that they too, were staring down Wally who wasn't sure where he was supposed to look. It was like all four nipples were fighting for his attention, flirting with him, beckoning him.

"When was the last time you titty-fucked someone?"

Wally turned his attention from the enormous breasts to Potey who continued to stare ahead at the show and had asked the question out of the corner of his mouth, unaware or uncaring that the stripper gyrating a few feet in front of them had likely heard the question, though she gave no indication that she had.

"Potey, I don't--"

"Come on. I'm serious. Answer the question. When was the last time you titty-fucked a fat chick?"

Wally turned his attention back to the naked flesh in front of him as an uneasy feeling reverberated in the pit of his stomach. He'd had it since they had walked in forty-five minutes earlier when he got his first glimpse of a stripper performing in the dimly-lit theater. It had started in his chest and slowly made its way through his body to where it now settled as low as it could go. The woman on stage swung her legs in front of her and sat back so each stilettoed-heel settled in front of Wally and Potey, her shaved crotch positioned equidistant between them. Wally could swear he could hear Potey giggling next to him.

"I'm going to hit the head." Wally stood up and rearranged his sad erection through his jeans--not bothering to try to hide the action from the other patrons. He slid out between the rows of swivel chairs and spotted two of Potey's friends who had joined them at the club--neither of which Wally had ever met. The two young men stood out among the other strip club patrons--pathetic-looking and disheveled older men whose best days were behind them.

In contrast, Jack was baby-faced, a tall hipsterish guy with a faux-hawk wearing a fitted shirt that accentuated his lean body. He was chatting up a dancer wearing a yellow ribbon on the side of her head that matched her bikini bottom. She was in the seat next to Jack and was leaning over, her bare breasts grazing his upper arm as she tossed her head and laughed haughtily. Potey's other friend, Adam, had his hands full, literally, as he palmed the breasts of a petite Asian woman giving him a lap dance. She straddled his legs with her back to him and was rocking back and forth, rubbing on top of his crotch. She kept looking over her shoulder seductively at Adam, a shaggy blonde wearing a polo shirt, cargo shorts and dirty flip flops, encouraging him to keep the twenties flowing.

Wally sidestepped the pair and made his way to the bathroom. Inside, a red bulb served as the only light, making it an easy transition from the dimly lit main room. Wally turned on the faucet and splashed tepid water on his face. He felt the blood rush away, both cooling and calming him.

"What the fuck are you doing, Wally Drummond?" he said as he looked at his reflection in the mirror. His shirt was disheveled and untucked, and his hair was unwashed and uncombed. His face sported three-day old stubble. His whole appearance made him look like an out-of-work soap opera actor. How did he let Potey talk him into coming? How pathetic was he? First he hit the bottle. Now he was leering at sad women who were being paid to rub themselves on him. He was moving from one tired cliché to the next. No, this wouldn't do.

The door opened and Potey's friend Jack stepped inside. He smiled at Wally as he pushed up his sleeves and stood in front of the urinal. He let out a sigh as Wally heard a heavy stream hit the back of the porcelain.

"You know, they really should put the urinals on the ceiling," Jack said, staring straight ahead as he relieved himself.

Wally turned his head and squinted. He pulled a paper towel from the rack and started to dry his hands. "I don't know what to say to that."

Jack laughed as he stepped away from the urinal. "The wall is disgusting in here. Lonely dudes at full salute would have better aim if they raised the target."

Wally shook his head and discarded the towel in a wastebasket behind the door, letting a smile cross his face. Jack's face joined Wally's in the mirror, the two guys staring at their reflections.

"I don't know why I'm even here," Wally said, taking a step back from the sink. "Fuckin' Potey."

"I know. It's a little depressing in there."

"Right?" Wally was relieved he wasn't the only one in the group who was uncomfortable.

"I just don't get strip clubs," Jack said as he dried his hands with a brown paper towel. "But Potey likes coming here, so I take one for the team." Wally nodded as Jack continued. "You know, it's Friday night--albeit a little early--but there's what like ten dudes out there? It's telling that between you, me, Adam and Potey, we're thirty percent of the crowd tonight."

"Thirty percent of the crowd but ninety percent of the teeth," Wally added.

Jack laughed a big hearty laugh and clapped his hand on Wally's shoulder. "I know, right?" he said. "It's like everyone's social security checks all came in the mail today."

The two men chuckled.

You're a funny dude," Jack continued. "I can see why

Potey likes you." Wally hadn't noticed before but Jack had a slight accent, pronouncing his er's as soft a's and elongating his vowels.

"You must've known Potey from Boston," Wally said.

"Yep. We were roommates at BU. And then we met up again when I moved out here a few years ago. He kept me grounded when I was settling in." Jack paused as he threw a paper towel in the trash. "Potey's not a bad guy." Wally bit his lip trying to picture Potey being helpful to anyone. Jack must have noticed the thought bubble above Wally's head and laughed again. "Really. He's rough around the edges but he's a good guy. I wouldn't go into battle with anyone else. No matter what shit I was going through."

Wally nodded and took a step toward the door, but Jack stopped him. "Let's walk outside for a little smoke, shall we?"

The pair exited the bathroom, and Jack motioned across the room to Potey that they'd be right outside. Potey nodded and waved him away dismissively as the two women with gigantic breasts danced in front of him. Wally and Jack made their way through the front of the club, past the bouncers and onto the sidewalk and into the heart of North Beach surrounded by dive bars, adult video stores and strip clubs. A few pizza joints broke up the hedonism, and the Beat Museum on the corner added some culture. The sidewalk was crowed--it was a Friday night--with groups of frat guys and day laborers roaming between establishments. A pair of cops on motorcycles sat across the street at the corner of Broadway and Kearney, lazily eyeing the scene, looking for someone to step out of line so they could arrest him for being drunk and disorderly, fill their quota for the night and go home.

Jack nudged Wally in the arm and motioned to an alley across the street that climbed toward the crest of Telegraph Hill. The pavement was so steep that the corner building's first and second floors were both at street level. Jack dashed across Broadway toward the alley with Wally looking each way before trailing behind. Jack stopped half-way up the alley and took a glass pipe and lighter out of his jeans pocket. A nugget of marijuana was stashed in the bowl. He offered it to Wally who shoved his hands in his pocket and shook his head. Jack shrugged and took a hit, being careful to blow the distinct-smelling smoke uphill away from Wally.

"How'd you meet Potey?" Jack asked before taking another hit. Wally looked down, waiting for Jack to finish.

"My wife. Potey was her band's manager."

Jack's eyebrows shot up as he picked a piece of ash from his lips. "Ahh, yes. Sunset Revolution."

Wally nodded as Jack continued.

"I may have seen one of their shows. Did they ever play at Red Devil Lounge on--ah, Polk Street?"

Wally shrugged his shoulders. "Maybe. Actually, I'm sure they did."

"I remember they had a woman bassist. Your wife?" Wally nodded as Jack continued. "And they're the band that is their own opening band, right?"

Wally smiled. "Yeah. Mister Roger's Coke Dealer."

"Fuckin' brilliant. They essentially ensure they won't be upstaged by the opening act."

Wally laughed. "It's more than that. It gave them a

chance to be themselves rather than that corporate rock bullshit the label turned them into."

Jack brought the pipe up to his lips and lit the weed as he took in another deep breath. He closed his eyes and held in the smoke for a few seconds before blowing it skyward.

"You sure you don't want a hit of this?"

Wally shook his head again. "I'm sure. Thanks."

They stood in silence for a few moments as Jack waited for the drug to take hold. Wally leaned against a mural on the side of the building painted to depict life in Chinatown which was just a few blocks away. Across the alley hung a black sign with white neon lettering spelling out "Basque Hotel". Wally could see a busy after work bar scene through the door.

"Did Sunset Revolution break up?"

The question took Wally by surprise. Jack seemed to sense the confusion and said, "Earlier you said that Potey was the band's manager, not is the band's manager. I'm a writer. I pay attention to tenses."

Wally breathed a little easier.

"Julie died a few months ago."

"I'm sorry, man. I didn't--"

"It's ok."

"Well, sorry to hear it."

The closest street light was down on Broadway but there was still enough light for Wally to see that Jack's eyes were now bloodshot and his facial features were more animated. His eyes darted this way and that, but Wally wasn't sure if the weed had stimulated him or had just made him paranoid.

"I've known Potey for fifteen years. This--" Jack motioned across the street toward the strip club. "--this has Potey's fingerprints all over it. It must have been his idea to try to make you feel better."

"It seems that way." Wally shuffled his feet. "I guess that a lot of my friends are trying to help."

"He did the same thing when my Dad passed away last year."

"Potey doesn't seem to have a lot of tricks up his sleeve."

The two men laughed.

"How are you doing, if you don't mind me asking?"

"As good as expected, I guess," Wally responded. "It's hard though, being a widower. Lots of things sneak up on you."

"What do you mean?"

"Well, like how do you tell people that Julie has passed? And who do I tell? Like the bartender at the bar we'd go to all the time. We had this rapport whenever we'd walk in and-- Is it my responsibility to tell him? What about the pharmacist at the Walgreens across the street. The dry cleaner? The guys at the deli who teased her about her avocado and sprout sandwiches?"

Jack smiled. "Yeah, I'd never think about that. It's a pickle. I guess you have to focus on the details like that to avoid thinking too much."

"Yeah, I'm just trying to stay busy. Work helps keep my mind off things."

Jack took a seat on the stairs leading up the sidewalk and motioned for Wally to join him.

"What kind of business you in?" Jack asked as Wally sat down.

"Sales. Software sales."

"Yeesh. Must be boring. How can you busy yourself doing sales?"

"It's not bad." Wally turned his hands over in his lap, one on top of the other. He stared toward the line of people passing along Broadway. They seemed happy and inebriated, pleased to be out and about.

"I'm a writer," Jack said matter-of-factly.

"You mentioned that." Wally could tell that Jack enjoyed telling people his profession, as if being a writer was impressive.

"Potey didn't tell you about my novel?" Jack continued. "It's the seventy-five thousand, three hundred and sixty-seventh best seller on Amazon dot com. Although I did win an award for having the best opening lines of any novel published that year."

Wally turned to face Jack and saw that he was being self-deprecating, but he also saw a hint of truth, like the lack of commercial success despite some critical acclaim was really eating him up. Wally decided to throw him a bone.

"Ok. I'll bite. Let's hear it."

Jack's face lit up. He stood up, straightened his posture like he was giving a reading at the local Barnes and Noble and proceeded to quote his own book: "'Jack and Dean tumbled out of the faded, weather-stained Victorian in San Francisco's Haight-Ashbury neighborhood on a Thursday afternoon, the streets still crowded with tourists and neighborhood types. It was what Jack liked to call a Full House Day: sunny, cloudless, a perfect day to drive a shiny red convertible over the Golden Gate Bridge and hang out with Danny, Uncle Jesse, Kimmie Gibler and the Olsen twins.'"

Wally clapped while Jack took a bow.

"Anyway," Jack continued. "Potey was instrumental in getting me to publish the book. Him and a few other people. Regardless of my lack of sales the process was cathartic. It let me move on. Without Potey I'd be stuck in place. He moves people forward in his own weird way."

Wally nodded.

"My advice--" Jack stood up, pocketing the pipe and lighter. "--is to just go with it. See where he takes you. If nothing works out the worst thing that happens is that you have a good story to tell." He reached down, offering Wally his hand. Wally took it and pulled himself up. "Maybe he'll lead you to the mother of all sales."

Wally grinned. "I don't see how--"

"--shit! Is that Potey and Adam?"

Jack was pointing down the alley and across the street where two men were splayed out on the ground in front of the strip club. Two other men, in baggy shirts, monstrous jeans and New York Yankee baseball caps, were repeatedly kicking them while a few others were holding back the bouncer. One of the guys on the ground wore a yellow shirt just visible underneath a blue sports coat.

"Yes, that's Potey," Wally exclaimed as he bounded down the stairs two at a time. He flew across the street, feeling Jack just behind him. As he got closer, Wally could see that the heavy-set man kicking Potey had short cropped hair under his hat and was wearing a long black trench coat. Without thinking, Wally launched himself at the hulking man, hoping his momentum was enough to knock him back or stun him while they could collect Potey and Adam and make their escape.

11

Everything slowed down as he flew through the air. The colorful neon signs reflecting off the sides of the building and the sidewalk. The gaping faces of the rubberneckers. Potey flinching through cracked and bleeding lips. The MLB logo on the man's cap. The bouncer desperately trying to break up the fight. Potey's attacker looked up and made eye contact with Wally, and his eyes grew wide as Wally's shoulder hit him in the ribs. The man let out a groan as Wally knocked him through the club's open front door. Wally's momentum sent him through the door as well, and he landed and rolled over the man who was tangled in his long black trench coat. Wally slammed his elbow into the man's temple--or where he thought the man's temple would be--and then stood and hurdled over him back onto the sidewalk. Jack had the other attacker in a headlock as Potey and Adam struggled to stand. The guys who were holding the bouncer stopped struggling with him and just stood there, apparently too shocked to react.

. . .

Wally heard commotion behind him and turned to see that Jack had thrown his adversary to the ground. Adam and Potey were already up and coming his way.

"Let's get the fuck out of here," Wally yelled and crashed through the crowd that had formed.

Wally led the four men in a dead sprint down Broadway toward Kearney Street where the North Beach neighborhood gave way to the Financial District. They continued across the street and ducked into a small alley marked Roland Street. Wally came to a stop, realizing he'd led them down a dead-end. He turned to look behind him, but it was too late to turn back as four pursuers lumbered into the alley.

Wally noticed the large man in the Yankees cap and trench coat who he had previously tackled through the doorway of the strip club was heading his way. The man didn't look like he was open to negotiation.

Adrenaline surging through his body, Wally held up his fists like he'd seen in so many movies. He circled his opponent, as the two sized each other up. The element of surprise had previously given Wally an advantage, and he hoped he had one more trick up his sleeve. The man opposite him had at least eighty pounds if not more on him. Wally would have to strike first.

Sounds of scuffling were all around them as the two continued to circle each other, arms up in a fighters' stance. Wally counted to himself. Three. Two. One. He lunged forward and struck the guy on the side of the head, his fist glancing off the man's temple. Wally stumbled forward and caught his balance, being sure to get his arms up, ready for the counter strike. The man laughed and reared back. Wally caught sight of a fist approaching his face, and everything went black.

12

Wally huddled in the snow, flakes swirling around him, the wind punching through his layers of clothing, chilling him, causing his bones to ache. It was dark and he was alone. Wet seeped up through his boots and soaked the bottom of his overcoat. A layer of frost and crusted ice lined the outside layer. Pain seared through his forehead, the cold stabbing his temple like a frozen knife. Wally felt the energy and warmth leaving his body, slowly leaking out and disappearing into the cold, dark night. Something was off, though. Wally strained his ears, focusing on notes being carried by the wind. It got louder as Wally focused, suddenly realizing it was a Reggae tune. "We're sick and tired of the ism and skism game." The dense air around Wally began to disperse, and the snow slowed. "Lord we know when we understand. Almighty God is a livin' man." The sky started to lighten and his feet and legs grew warm. "You can fool some people sometimes. But you can't fool all the people all the time. So now we see the light. We gonna stand up for our right."

. . .

Wally opened his eyes. He was lying down on a black leather couch in a bright room. Familiar voices and loud laughing echoed off the bare, white walls, and the music from his dream continued to play in the background.

Get up. Stand up. Stand up for your right.

Get up. Stand up. Don't give up the fight.

There was a whiff of marijuana smoke in the room. Wally did an assessment of his body parts. Toes. Check. Kneecaps. Check. Ribs. Check. Head. Strangely numb. He shifted his neck a bit and heard rustling by his ear. He shifted again, and a bag of frozen peas slid off the side of his face, falling onto the floor.

"Wall-seph!" came a booming voice from across the room. "You're alive."

Potey's face appeared above Wally. He was still wearing the blue sports coat, though it was torn at the shoulder, a sliver of yellow showing through. He was also grinning a silly little grin and was motioning to some other people. Preceded by a puff of smoke, Jack's and Adam's faces appeared next to Potey's.

"Hey, little buddy. You did all right," Jack said, matching Potey's grin.

"How's that face?" Adam craned his neck to get a better look.

"Looks like you're going to have a great big shiner," Potey said with a hint of pride in his voice.

Wally closed his eyes. These morons' faces weren't exactly the view he wanted to see as he drifted back into consciousness. He had a slew of questions but couldn't settle on which one to ask first.

Jack seemed to sense the confusion. "That was a nice

punch you threw back there," he said. "You kept that guy busy long enough for us to take care of the others. Once he knocked you out--and man, did he knock you out--he saw he was outnumbered and high-tailed it out of there. Was that your first punch ever?"

Wally nodded.

"No shit?" Adam exclaimed. His sandy hair covered his forehead, lightly brushing up against his dark eyebrows. "You just popped your punch cherry?" Jack and Potey high-fived as Wally grinned. Wally closed his eyes and waved the jubilant victors away.

"Yes, you sleep, Wall-a-saurus. Dream about the hurt you put on those mother-fuckers."

Wally heard the trio scamper back across the room followed by the distinctive bubbling of bong water. He shifted on the well-worn couch cushions and touched the bruise on the side of his head. It was tender but the cold had numbed any pain he should have been feeling. Pain. The emptiness came rushing back, the memories of his struggles and grief of the past few months. His drinking. Demons in the form of what ifs and should have beens swirled through his dream state, haunting him, not letting him forget that he was a loser, a cad, lonely without hope. His temples were pounding now, and Wally buried his head in his arms, curling up into the fetal position, settling into a troubled sleep.

13

The booming voice came over the speakerphone, demanding an update on the latest sales numbers. Trembling, Wally shuffled through his notebook, frantically turning each page, trying in vain to find the information expected of him. Murmurs floated up from around the table. A stifled laugh turned into a cough. A patronizing sigh. Impatient whispers. He could feel his face turn pink, red, then crimson. The shame overpowering, Wally hung his head, suddenly noticing he wasn't wearing any pants. His penis just lay there, flaccid, squeezed between his thighs, pale and pathetic. No one seemed to notice. They were all averting their eyes due to his conference call faux pas, letting him figuratively twist in the wind when in fact he was quite literally hung out to dry. 'Fuck it,' he whispered and stood up, revealing himself to the room. A gasp. Arched eyebrows. A low whistle. Wally banged his fist on the table. 'Enough!'

. . .

The elevator door opened, and Wally stepped out into the reception area. For the first time in months, he was wearing a suit to work, neatly pressed, shirt tucked in, sneakers left at home in his closet. He'd woken up late, splayed out on Jack's black leather couch. Overnight, the bag of peas had split open, spilling the warm, squishy mess all over the cushions, Wally's body and his clothes. Potey's friend Jack had been cool about it, tossing Wally a roll of paper towels on his way out the door.

"No worries," he'd shouted over his shoulder as he left for work. "It's an old couch."

Wally had cleaned up the best he could given the sparse supplies at hand and had made his way back to his apartment and a nice, warm shower. His head had pounded as he let the water beat against his chest. He'd breathed in the rising steam, taking it in through his nose in long, deep breaths, soothing his nasal cavities and lungs.

After his shower, he'd inspected his eye in the bathroom mirror, turning his face this way and that, trying to get a closer view of the damage done to his face. His eye had puffed up, and he could barely see through his swollen, greenish-blue lids. It looked kind of badass, Wally had thought as he touched the skin.

Never in a million years would Julie have believed that he'd gotten into a fight, much less connected a punch against a considerably bigger adversary. As he'd stared at his face in the mirror, Wally fantasized about recounting the fight to her in every detail: the strip club, the wandering areolas, how he tackled the guy who was kicking Potey and how he led them down a dead-end alley. Julie would laugh, he decided, tickling him behind his ear before pinning him to the mattress and having her way with him.

Julie would've then told Wally to stop sulking, to own his misfortune and his embarrassing mark. So, Wally had dusted off one of his suits and put it on, hoping that coworkers would be too distracted by his dapper clothes to ask about his new accessory, a black eye patch that he pulled from an old pirate costume that Julie had gotten for Joey a few years back. He stood in front of the floor length mirror in his bedroom, admiring his new look: Captain Bluebeard on his way to his cousin's bar mitzvah. The punk in Julie would've loved it.

Twenty minutes later as he strode through his office's reception area, the suit and eye patch gave Wally an air of confidence he hadn't felt in a long time. Rather than shuffle past his coworkers, head down, hoping no one would try to initiate conversation or ask him the dreaded, "How are you doing?" question, Wally walked chin up, made eye contact with Jeffrey, the receptionist, and passed through the glass door that led into a massive cubicle farm.

Measuring more than six thousand square feet and taking up the entire fourteenth floor of a glass and steel skyscraper in the Financial District, the bullpen was where three hundred salespeople at Wally's company hit the phones, cajoling, needling, begging IT managers around the world to take a briefing or watch a demo of the company's latest enterprise software. Streamline operations, Embrace digital transformation, Be more agile came tumbling out of their mouths, through their VoIP headsets, across fiber, into the cloud and back out again.

They were taught that if a yes wasn't achieved within fifteen seconds of initiating the call it was a lost cause. Time to disengage, cut the bullshit and hang up. Someone else, more susceptible to hype could be behind the next phone number on their list. The more numbers their computers could dial, the more sales could be won. Truly a spray and pray approach.

Wally had been what the sales managers liked to call a burner--someone who could go through an entire call sheet before lunch, churning through leads like a barber cutting hair. He had a knack for knowing within a few words whether it was worth his time to continue. If his intuition told him to move on, he did, often without saying goodbye, hanging up in midsentence if need be. Then on to the next call, spouting his well-honed script while listening intently for that sigh, that stutter or that tone that told him everything he needed to know.

Wally passed a group of men and women huddled around a cubicle. They cupped steaming coffee mugs and held half-eaten muffins, bullshitting for a few moments before the rush. The chatter died down as Wally strode by, and they exchanged inquisitive glances.

"Ahoy, Captain," teased a young man who had poked his head out of the next cube as Wally passed, his arm raised, fist clinched. "Working a half day today?"

"Argh!" Wally exclaimed as he passed, making sure the young man knew that Wally wasn't fazed by the joke. The man laughed and gave Wally a nod before getting back on the phone.

It was three minutes past eight o'clock, meaning it was just after eleven in New York when IT managers at thousands of companies on Wall Street, in Mid-Town and across the river in Brooklyn would be winding down their morning and start to coast toward lunchtime. It was prime calling time for a burner like Wally, and normally, on a typical day, he'd be sitting at his desk, headset on, working his way through his call sheet. Beads of sweat would be forming around his hairline and his golf shirt would be damp from the intense concentration it took to dial number after number and try to persuade people he'd never met that he knew exactly what they needed to optimize their workflows, streamline their supply chain or improve the customer experience. The several dozen calls he'd make each hour would only turn into two or three solid leads, but it was a volume business, and the leads added up until Wally eventually found himself at the top of the sales leaderboard, his name written so long ago in black ink on the whiteboard that it eventually faded blue.

It hadn't been like that recently. Ever since Julie died, he'd been going through the motions. He'd be lucky to get to the office by ten, way too late to make calls to the lucrative New York market and having to call the middle of the country. He was lucky to get through a single call sheet in a day, cutting his chances of making a sale and a commission by a third, seeing his name tumbling from the top of the leaderboard to somewhere in the middle.

But today. Today was different. He felt confident again. His old self. Adrenaline surged through his body as he caught sight of his desk across the bullpen, quickening his pace. Wally slung his backpack over his chair and booted up his computer. No time to get a glass of water in the kitchen. It was time to sell.

Wally sat in his chair and squinted at his computer

screen. The pixels that made up the words and numbers on screen were blurred, his eyesight still not adjusted to his single lens view. Wally grinned and whipped off the eye patch, revealing the gruesome wound underneath.

"Fuck it," Wally whispered and affixed his headset around his ear. "Time to sell."

14

Xander's face was frozen, mouth open, tonsils reverberating, lips cracked and spread tight. He was struggling to hit the high note, but the crowd seemed to be giving him an A for his effort. Julie was up onstage doing her thing as well--arms, hands and drumsticks a blur as she banged away on her kit. The song was coming to a crescendo and she was working hard, bringing everyone slowly toward climax and the money shot. The bassist hit his last note and Julie reared back to give her cymbal a mighty strike. Sparks flew as she made contact, exploding in a fountain of red, yellow and blue flames.

A curtain behind the stage caught fire and quickly engulfed the entire back wall. Panic spread through the crowd as Wally was pushed backward toward the door. He could see Julie still on stage, her clothes on fire, arms still flailing away, drumming, drumming away.

Someone's fist hit Wally in the side of the head and a young woman wearing clown makeup screamed for him to get out of the way. He fell to his knees, and someone pushed him down further. Heavy footsteps rained down on his body as he *shielded his head, screaming Julie's name. His leg started to burn, and he noticed he was on fire, the flames licking his bright green Saucony shoes. Everything went black as he was kicked in the head, never to regain consciousness.*

"Hey, mate, you ok?"

A hand went up in front of Wally's face, snapping him out of his waking nightmare. Up on stage, the rock-folk duo The Deserters wailed through their hit song "Eyes on the Horizon" as a single spotlight shown down on the two brothers from the South, a clean-cut guitarist and an unkempt banjo player, the new darlings of the alternative scene. Wally had heard of them only briefly--Julie had apparently been a fan--and Julie's bandmate Xander had dragged him to this show in Berkeley. Apparently, Xander had gone in with Julie on the tickets earlier in the year, and he felt that it was his duty to extend the invitation to Wally. Julie would have wanted it this way, he said over the phone, and Wally was too tired to argue.

"I'm fine," Wally responded now as he swatted Xander's hand away from his face. "I was just getting into the music."

Xander smiled. "I told ya you'd like 'em."

It had been three weeks since the fight in the alleyway, and Wally's eye had almost fully healed. The swelling had gone down and only a splatter of greenish-yellow remained.

No one at his office had said a thing when he'd walked off the elevator the day after he'd gotten punched. A few gave him second glances but most just averted their eyes, stared at the floor or Wally's belt buckle and moved on. People were walking on egg shells around him and maybe assumed that his injury was some sadistic part of the grieving process. Had he gotten drunk and fallen down the stairs? Was he a member of some underground fight club? Perhaps Wally had picked a fight with a professional kickboxer in some sadistic way to punish himself. He imagined them whispering in the conference room, and Wally got a kick out of the fact that the rumors were probably much more interesting than the truth.

Since he took off the ridiculous eyepatch in his cubicle the day after the fight, Wally took no pains to cover up his badge of honor. Instead of hiding the wound, the mild-mannered software salesman left it open to view--often weeping, with pus leaking out of the corner of his eye as it healed. He got off on the way it made his co-workers uncomfortable--especially during long conference calls--and relished that no one dared mention it. He was like the Emperor with no clothes and no one had the balls to tell him he was walking around naked.

The last few notes eked out of the instruments and the crowd erupted. Some began to chant the band's name, urging them to come back for an encore. The lights in the gallery remained off, so it was obvious to Wally that there would be another set. He and Xander stood there in silence, facing the stage, hands in their pockets.

"Who was the opening band?" Wally finally asked. He saw Xander shrug his shoulders in his periphery vision.

"Dunno. I never catch the opening band."

"Oh."

Xander turned to face Wally and asked, "Did Julie ever tell you why we started Mister Roger's Coke Dealer?"

Wally shook his head.

"It was her idea. Sunset Revolution was just starting to make some noise, and the record label wanted us to change our stage presence. Ditch the grunge and start wearing shirts and comb our hair. Nigel, our former manager, tried to push back, but the suits were comin' on real hard. They had us out to be the next Coldplay or some shit like that. Julie fought it. Man, did she fight it. She said she got into music to express herself, and corporate rock wasn't going to mesh with her beliefs. We were all like, chill, Julie, this is our big break. Don't fuck with it."

Xander paused to chuckle before continuing.

"Anyway, we were sitting around having this meeting, just the band and Nigel, and finally Julie says that we should go in the opposite direction and become less attractive to the label. She started talking about going punk, wearing torn clothing, painting our faces. It was so ridiculous that we started chiming in. Paint our nails black, set fire to our instruments, sacrifice animals on stage. We were really getting into it. But suddenly I got this feeling that Julie wasn't joking. She actually wanted to do all these things--"

"Excuse me," came a voice from behind them. They turned to see a group of young women in their mid-twenties sitting one row back. The woman in the middle wearing a tight white tank top held out her hand. "You're Xander from Sunset Revolution, aren't you?"

Wally smirked and Xander demurred. He put his head down before finally giving an affirmative. As soon as he gave that sign, the four women started to fidget excitedly, patting down their clothes, twittling with their hair.

"Xander Pruitt." He shook the woman's hand half-heartedly.

"I'm Angie. Sorry to hear about your bassist. So tragic."

"So sad," another woman chimed in.

Xander shook his head and placed his hand on Wally's forearm, silently apologizing for the intrusion--a gesture unnoticed by the women but greatly appreciated by the young widower.

The women just giggled and started pulling out their phones. "Can we get a picture with you?" Angie asked. Xander motioned for the group to gather around him in a pose, and one woman passed her phone to Wally. The gaggle pressed in around Xander and turned on their smiles. Other concertgoers were starting to crane their necks to see who was getting their picture taken, desperately searching their memories, trying to determine which celebrity was in their midst. Wally lined up the shot and pressed a button, freezing time for an instant before the phone reverted back to active camera mode. He passed the phone back to the woman and turned to Xander. Their prey bagged, the women gathered around the phone to make sure their hair was appropriate enough to be tagged on Facebook.

"How are you doing," Xander asked, leaning in to Wally.

"Ok."

"Really?" Xander arched his eyebrows. "You can do better than that."

Wally sighed. "Yeah, ok. Not good, but getting better. Work is picking up."

"That old killer sales instinct coming back?"

"Yeah, it feels almost normal for a few hours."

Xander nodded as Wally continued. "Listen, I'd give anything for Julie to be here instead of me right now."

"Me too, mate. Me too."

Wally gave him a look. "I bet. Per my wishes, you guys would be together."

Xander hesitated, then seemed to catch Wally's meaning.

"Oh right," he said, smirking. "If you had been the one to die, I'd be dating Julie right now. That's what you wanted, right?"

Wally sighed. "I know. Sounds creepy when you look at it from the perspective of what actually did happen."

"Dude, it's always been creepy. And honestly, I wouldn't have followed through with your weird little plan."

Wally arched his eyebrow.

"Seriously," Xander continued. "It's not like you would have been able to complain."

Both men laughed and turned to face the stage, anticipating the band coming back out, lost in their own thoughts about Julie.

"So, anyway," Xander turned back to Wally who nodded. "The label is just pissing off all of us. Julie said that we should just say fuck it and become an opening band, a joke, a band that other bands hired to make them look good. We all laughed, but Julie was serious. She started whispering to Nigel and then revealed this crazy idea to become our own opening band. Immediately, we knew we had to do it. If not for our own sake but for Julie's. Without Mister Rogers she would've been miserable, a mess. From then on we knew that there'd be no Sunset Revolution without Mister Rogers' Coke Dealer."

"And the rest is history," Wally quipped. He hadn't heard

the story. In fact, he'd never thought to ask. He just assumed that the two bands had formed at the same time rather than one begetting the other.

"Julie really was that punk chick on stage," Xander said. "She loved banging on that old drum set of hers. It was obvious to us all that she detested what Sunset Revolution was becoming."

Wally turned his head up to the ceiling and exhaled deeply. "The first time I saw Julie, you guys were up on stage playing as Mister Roger's Coke Dealer. That was the Julie I fell in love with, the one that wore her hair in pigtails and wore cartoon T-shirts. Not some cleaned up act."

Xander put his hands up to Wally's face, turned his head and looked directly at his black eye.

"Julie," he said, "Would've absolutely loved this shiner of yours."

He patted Wally on the shoulder just as the lights on stage dimmed and the roadies ducked behind the curtains. Smiling and shaking his head, Wally cupped his hands to his face and let loose with a high-pitched "Wooooooo!". Xander nodded, clapped his hands and gave a shout as The Deserters came on for their encore.

15

One flinch. One decisive move. That's all it would take. Wally could end it all, right here. All he had to do was jerk the wheel, aim for the side of the Caldecott Tunnel running under the Berkeley Hills, and end his suffering in a single, fiery crash.

Wally pulled up to the small, single story ranch house at the end of the street, slamming the gears into neutral before shutting down the engine.

Despite having less than 20,000 miles on it, Julie's old 1996 Jeep Wrangler was a wreck. Its lightly rusted exterior, paint job worn thin by salty air on the coast, bald tires, a ratty soft top torn open in several break-ins and more door dings than one could count made it seem like it had been heavily used, maybe driven across-country a few times. It hadn't. Julie'd gotten it as a graduation gift from her parents, but, with little use for it in the city, the car had simply been shuffled from block to block around various neighborhoods to avoid street sweeping for the past 15 years. Wally doubted that Julie had driven it more than 20 miles in a single trip.

Wally's gaze wandered past the front walk, up the three concrete steps and to the red paneled door, a faded, drooping mourning wreath nailed to its front, guarding the entrance. On cue, it opened, and Julie's mom peered out, her short, blond bob filling the doorway.

"Hey, Bonnie," Wally said as he exited the jeep and strode up the walkway. "How're you?"

Bonnie smiled, took one step outside and waved Wally inside. "We're taking it one day at a time. The good Lord never intended parents to outlive their child."

Wally nodded and stepped inside, his eyes taking a few seconds to adjust to the dim lighting. Julie's stoic father Nate came into focus sitting in his recliner in the corner of the living room. A college football game on TV cast shadows across his weathered face, with wrinkles more pronounced than the last time Wally had seen him just a few months earlier at the funeral. A tall wicker bookcase filled the entirety of the opposite wall, and it was occupied, not with books, but with the mementos and detritus of a typical family: dozens of framed photos, knick-knacks from a vacation to Disneyland and scattered trinkets of everyday life--a ball of yarn with threaded needle, a pile of forgotten receipts, a few old crossword puzzles. More unframed dog-eared photos were taped to the sides of the bookcase, impromptu poses of Julie and her parents laughing, hugging and holding each other tight.

"Wally."

Julie's father stood and held out his hand. Wally took it

and accepted the firm grip, shaking it lightly, the closest thing he'd ever gotten to a hug out of the man.

"Nate, get the boy a beer. You want a beer, Wally?"

"I'd love one," Wally responded, surprised by his own answer. He'd expected a quick in and out, to give them what he'd brought for them and then take off.

Nate nodded and headed through an archway leading to the kitchen. Wally took his customary place at the end of the couch, far from the TV. Bonnie looked down at Wally, shaking her head, her hands on her hips, a worried look on her face.

"You look thin, dear. Are you eating?"

"Yeah, I'm doing alright. In fact, the fellows in the taqueria down the street know me by name."

"Oh, honey, you need more than burritos in your diet. Let me heat you up some chicken parm. It'll just be a minute."

Wally shook his head. "No, thanks. I actually need to take off soon. I can't leave Joey at home too long or he pisses on the couch."

Bonnie frowned. "You sure?"

"I'm sure."

"Ok, but I'm telling your mother you look thin. You know we talk quite often. She was so fond of our little Julie."

Wally nodded. He knew that Julie had had a better relationship with his mother than he had with his.

"I have a box of Julie's things in the car. In fact, I came to drop off the car as well. I thought Alice could use it. No use for it in the city. Not sure why we held onto it this long. I'll just ask for a ride to BART in a bit."

"That's really nice of you to want to give it to Julie's cousin. She's going to need a vehicle when she heads to

UCLA in the Fall. But are you sure you don't want to keep it? Don't you need something to help you get around?"

Wally shook his head. "No thanks, Bonnie. Honestly, the car is more trouble than it's worth. I just take the bus or Uber."

Nate came back into the living room with two silver Coors Lite cans and held one out to Wally. Condensation was forming, and it chilled Wally's hand as he opened it. He held the can in Nate's direction, making eye contact, and Julie's dad did the same. They both took a sip, then turned their attention to the game on TV.

Bonnie sighed. "I guess I'll go take a look at that box you mentioned. The car's open?"

"The keys are in the ignition."

Bonnie nodded and opened the front door and stepped outside. The two men sat in silence for a few minutes, absent-mindedly watching the football game. Cal was losing to USC, which added to the melancholy mood. Wally sipped his beer quietly, keeping one eye on the clock, slowly ticking off the seconds, the sound of football washing over him. Wally smiled as he remembered something Julie had told him, that she hated football because it was the sound of her father ignoring her.

"I heard Bonnie trying to get you to eat," Nate said over the din. "I hope you don't mind. She just needs to mother again."

Wally looked away from the TV at Nate. "I know. I don't mind. I can't imagine what she's going through."

Nate nodded. "It helps to have someone to take care of. It gets her mind off things."

"Yep. I have Joey. Not sure what I'd do if he didn't keep

me on a schedule--which reminds me, I really do need to get back to the city, so if I could get that ride--"

Nate raised his beer can as if to put the request on hold.

"Relax, Wally. We just opened beers." He took a sip and returned his attention back to the game.

"I brought some stuff that belonged to Julie that I thought you'd like." Nate nodded without taking his gaze off the TV. "Some photos. Jewelry. A few drumsticks."

"She loved to drum," Nate finally responded. "It saved her."

It saved her. Now that piqued Wally's interest. It was said matter-of-factly, like Wally should know what was meant, but he couldn't help but wonder if it was an invitation to ask questions. Born in the late Sixties while coming of age in the Reagan Eighties, Nate was a counter to the counter-culture, conservative socially and politically, bound and determined to be mainstream, to be normal. He'd never volunteer information willingly, nor be the one to start up an uncomfortable conversation.

"Saved her? What do you mean?"

"Oh, you know. It gave her something to live for." Nate continued to fixate on the game in front of him as he spoke. He paused to let the sentence sink in, then, apparently satisfied with the weight of his words, he continued. "When Julie was a kid I'd come home from work and she'd be there to greet me at the door, big smile on her face, arms wide, the next half-hour till dinner all scheduled for us. We'd play Chinese Checkers or The Game of Life. Dress up. Or throw the ball around in the back. She'd chat away about her day, what she learned in school, what the teacher did, what the schoolyard gossip was. I'd tease her about boys, and she'd blush and declare she'd never get married."

He stole a glance at Wally as he said married then continued.

"It was the best part of my day, hands down. I'd leave the office all tired and stressed out, but I'd have a huge grin on my face by the time I pulled into the driveway. Anyway, as you can imagine, it didn't last. Julie got older, and she stopped greeting me at the door. I'd have to find her, usually in her room, laying on her bed, reading a book or doing homework. She was too busy to hang out with her old dad. And, I understood. She couldn't be my little girl forever. She'd grow up, become a woman. It just seemed to be going so fast."

Wally subconsciously shifted on the couch as Nate paused to take a long draught of his beer. Wally took a sip of his.

"One night, Bonnie told me that she was worried about Julie. That she seemed depressed. A teacher told her that Julie had become withdrawn at school. Had shrunk her group of friends to just a few girls. I told Bonnie that it sounded like typical teenager stuff. You know, sullen, angsty stuff that she'd grow out of. So this went on for a year, and then high school started, and I started to worry. That's when kids figure out who they are. Who their friends are. What defines them. Are they jocks? Or into theater? Or whatever. I didn't want this phase she was in to define the rest of her life. I felt I had to do something, so I got out this old CD player and let Julie set it up in her room. I had a few albums hangin' around. Springsteen, Pet Shop Boys, Paul Simon."

Wally stifled a laugh at the thought of his Jules singing "You Can Call Me Al".

"I'd come home, and she'd be in her room as usual, but there'd be music playing, and I swore I could hear her singin' along. Eventually, my old CDs were pushed aside and replaced by stuff that she'd bought. That's when she got into this punk stuff. You know, leather jackets, spikey hair, some group called the Dead Kennedys. She was wearing drab, dark clothing. Pierced her own ears with a safety pin.

Wally smiled. This was the Jules that he knew and fell in love with.

"Anyway, I really started to get worried when she came home in a patrol car one night. They'd caught her with spray paint down by the highway overpass. It was like she didn't care--about school, her future, herself."

"Luckily, she taught herself to play the guitar and then the drums and I guess you know the rest. Even back then I could see a change in her mood. Sure, she was still dark and weird, but she was excited about something. She cared. And that's all I really wanted.

"You don't think she would have hurt herself?" Wally asked, thinking back to his aborted attempt on the bridge.

"No. I don't think so," Nate responded.

Wally nodded in agreement, satisfied and relieved by his answer. Nate turned back to the game and tipped back his beer, emptying the can in one swig.

"Why are you telling me this?"

The old man turned back to Wally and looked him square in the eyes.

"You need to find something you care about, Wally. Pick up a new hobby. Get out of that small apartment."

"I am thinking about getting out of town for a while. San

Diego. Mexico. South America. Somewhere warm and beachy."

Nate stood up, placed his beer can on the table next to his chair and announced, "Good. Time to get you to BART. Let's go."

Wally stood up, and Nate took a step forward and embraced him, arms wrapped fully around Wally's body. Shocked, Wally froze, but as the hug continued, he placed his hands on Nate's back and gave the big man a squeeze. Nate pulled him in closer and buried his face in the nook between Wally's neck and shoulder. Wally swore he felt a shudder, perhaps a sob, but he wasn't sure. He just held on and rode out the hug as long as he could.

16

"Clean up on aisle six" echoed throughout the grocery store, bouncing off the hard tile floor before dissipating somewhere in the large empty space between the top of the shelves and the high ceiling. Wally looked up from the rows of Progresso Soup cans and took a step toward the end of the aisle, craning his neck to see the sign hanging above his head. His foot expected a dry surface but hit a wet patch, a syrupy condensed substance seeping out from underneath the shelves. As he tried to catch himself, he fell to the cold, hard concrete floor, and Wally caught a glimpse of the sign he was trying to read, a big red "6" flashing through his field of vision just before a sickening smack of his head caused him to lose consciousness.

"Wally?"

A woman with long black hair was standing in front of him, waving her hand, playfully trying to get Wally's attention. A little embarrassed that he was caught in one of his macabre day dreams, Wally flinched as he stood in the soup section, aisle six, holding the handles of his basket in both hands in front of him. The woman was wearing a purple tank top and black yoga pants. She was toned and her white flawless skin provided a sharp contrast with her colorful shirt and dark hair.

"Wally? It's Shannon. From Oracle."

The woman smiled uncertainly but in a kind way. Wally stuck out his hand, but she sidestepped his professional greeting, moving in closer, offering up her cheek as she leaned in. Wally gave it a quick peck, getting a noseful of what smelled like vanilla extract emanating off her neck while hoping his stubble wouldn't irritate her skin.

"You worked in customer service, right?" Wally asked as he took a step back. "Sixth floor?"

The woman smiled, relieved. That's right. I was on Nilesh's team. You still in sales?" She reached back with one arm to take hold of her cart and pull it closer to her, allowing another shopper to squeeze past them. Wally put his basket down on the tiled floor, spreading his feet so he could cradle it between his ankles.

"I'm over at Insignia now. Security software."

"And how is that going?"

"It's ok. Sales is sales, right?"

Shannon shrugged. "Is that all you're getting?" She motioned at Wally's basket on the floor. It was filled with canned goods, frozen foods and pre-made meals stuffed with preservatives. Shannon's cart on the other hand was overloaded with fresh fruits and vegetables, pastas and rice--raw ingredients that she would no doubt turn into healthy, delicious home-cooked meals.

"You're just a sack of flour away from starring in a Whole

Foods commercial," Wally quipped. Shannon laughed and bent over her cart to move some bags around. She pulled two wine bottles apart to reveal a white bag made of parchment with Gold Medal all-purpose flour written on the label.

"Where are the cameras? I'm ready for my close up, Mister DeMille." Shannon turned her face to show Wally her profile, holding her posture for a full two seconds before breaking character and cracking up. She laughed in short choppy guffaws as if trying to catch her breath between yoga poses. Wally waited as the chuckling continued, staring at this unexpected acquaintance from the past. Finally, Shannon caught herself, clasping her hand over her mouth, stifling the nervous laughter. "Sorry, I'm a little spazzy today. I just got out of yoga class, and I have a lot of energy. It's good energy, though, you know?"

"No worries. I wish I had a hobby or an exercise routine. I just walk my dog, eat bad food and watch TV."

"Your wife doesn't take care of you?"

Wally flinched and broke eye contact, looking around him furtively, searching for something to lock his sight onto. He spied a maple syrup display down the aisle a bit, rows and rows of Aunt Jemima and Mrs. Buttersworth staring back, goofy grins on their dark faces, dozens of smiles just off Shannon's left shoulder.

"She's, uh--" he stammered. "You see, we're no longer--"

"No need to explain," Shannon interrupted. The smile on her face had faded, but Wally could see the smile in her eyes grow brighter. "My neighbor just separated from his wife and all he eats is take out. Let me fix you a home cooked meal. Are you free tonight?"

"Yes." The words were blurted, almost spit out, surprising

Wally. Wally forced a smile, but his heart was pounding, and he shivered, feeling his skin grow cold and clammy. "Do you live in the neighborhood?"

"Yes. Just up the hill off Sacramento. Do you know Golden Court?"

"That pedestrian-only street?"

Shannon nodded.

"My dog and I walk down there all the time. The houses are so cool. And everyone's gardens. They're so lush. It's like you're not even in the city when you turn the corner."

"Yeah, I got lucky when I moved here back in the early Nineties. Gotta love rent control."

"Which building is yours?"

"Do you know the gigantic yucca plant on the left when you go down the stairs?"

"Uh huh."

"That's me. Apartment five."

"What time should I come over?"

Apparently pleased with herself, Shannon leaned her elbow on the edge of her shopping cart, seemingly trying to be cool or coy--or maybe both--but she must have forgotten that it was on wheels because the weight caused her cart to start rolling down the aisle. Shannon stumbled forward as the cart moved out from underneath her. She caught herself and smoothed out her pants, brushed back her long black hair behind her ears and straightened up, her arms pinned to her sides as if nothing had happened. The cart continued to roll down the aisle, and the wheels must've been a bit rusty because it veered off to the left directly toward the rows of syrup containers that had attracted Wally's attention a few moments before. Wally leapt forward but it was too late as the cart crashed into the display, knocking over several of the glass jars, one dangerously close to rolling off the shelf and crashing onto the floor. Luckily Wally was in position to catch the jar as it rolled to the edge. It fell into the palm of his hand as it dropped, and Wally casually repositioned it in its proper row.

"Oh, my god," Shannon said, covering her face with her hands. "I'm such a klutz. Here I am trying to play it cool--"

"It's fine," Wally interrupted her, reorganizing the syrup display. "No harm, no foul. Let's just sneak away before anyone notices."

Wally put his arm around Shannon, guiding her down the aisle toward her cart, his own basket filled with frozen burritos, Lean Cuisines and Kraft macaroni left on the floor under the watchful eyes of the Aunt Jemimas. As he pushed Shannon's cart toward the checkout line, the basket lay there behind him.

17

Several of the overhead luggage compartments flew open as the cabin tilted forward. Wally expected screams but it was deathly silent as if all two hundred passengers were resigned to their fate. The plane banked to the right and continued to dive. Wally suddenly noticed that he was clutching the hand of the woman next to him, and her fingernails were digging into his skin. He closed his eyes and...

Shannon peered across the table through the dimly-lit room making eyes at Wally. Her elbows were upright on the table with her arms coming together at her wrist, her chin resting on the backs of her hands, forming a teepee over her tomato-sauce streaked dinner plate. She was still clutching her napkin that was draped over her place setting despite having finished the main course forty-five minutes earlier, time forgotten as the two lost themselves in deep talk.

It had been a good conversation, nay a great conversation, Wally thought. As it turned out, Shannon and Wally had lived on the same block in the Haight--though several years apart. It had been their first apartment in the city for both of them, and they swapped stories about the crazy characters that hung out in the area. There was Cat Lady who fed all the neighborhood strays. There was Gap-Tooth and Orange Fleece, a guy who wore an orange fleece every day regardless of the weather or time of day. Wally's favorite was Jamison, a homeless man who unrolled his sleeping bag between the fire hydrant and bus stop sign in front of his building nearly every night. Wally would say hello or wave when he saw him and pass him a take-out container of leftovers when he could.

Every character had a quirk, and Jamison's was amazing. He spent most of his days downtown on Market Street panhandling for spare change, and his unprotected balding head would burn mercilessly. Rather than get a hat, Jamison would apply aloe lotion on his peeling scalp every night to cool the burn. He'd then rub the excess lotion on the bus stop sign, leaving an aromatic oil slick about two and a half feet off the ground that made all the neighborhood dogs go crazy. An unsuspecting owner would be coming down the street, and then their dog would dart across the sidewalk--jerking their owner's arm--and start sniffing and licking the pole.

Eventually, the paint had worn off, and people who lived nearby jokingly named it the Aloe Pole and made sure to linger a few moments when a dog walker came down the sidewalk. Shannon told Wally that Jamison eventually got a girlfriend, and she would rub the lotion on his head for him. Nevertheless, the woman still rubbed the excess lotion on the pole, keeping the tradition intact.

Throughout their conversation, Shannon was all smiles, her thin lips stretched tight across her teeth, skin taut across her cheekbones, pulling her ears down a few millimeters from their normal position next to her temples. She kept running her hands through her hair, pulling a few strands out of a twisted, haphazard braid that was held up by what looked like a tortoiseshell butterfly clip. Wally was sure he spotted a speck of red sauce in the corner of her mouth.

"Let me clean up," Wally said as he rose from the table.

"Let's do it together," Shannon responded, mirroring Wally's motions as the two collected plates and silverware and brought it into the kitchen.

"Wash or dry?"

"Why don't I wash? If I dry, I'll just put your dishes away in the wrong cabinet."

Wally turned on the faucet and squirted a drop of liquid soap on a sponge sitting on the sill above the sink. He waited for the temperature to go up and started to wipe food from a plate. After a quick rinse, he handed the dish to Shannon who gave it a good once over with a towel and placed it in a cabinet above her head. They repeated the process for the rest of the china, wordlessly but content. Wally's hand touched Shannon's a few times as they made an exchange, sending a jolt shooting up through his arm, the anticipation growing each time. He knew that she felt it too, her wide grin trembling at the corners of her mouth.

The last fork in hand, Wally delayed as long as he could, fumbling with the utensil under the faucet, deliberately going over every tong with the sponge, rubbing and scrubbing at phantom food particles. He wasn't sure if he wanted what he knew would come next. Shannon stood patiently to his side, towel in hand, ready to put the fork in its place in the drawer.

"I think it's clean," she whispered, putting her hand on

the small of Wally's back. She leaned in and took the fork from his hands, ran it under the water for a second and rubbed it dry. The sponge fell from Wally's grasp and he turned to face her. His hands were trembling, so he wiped them on his shirt and shoved them in his jeans pockets. He straightened his arms, pushing his hands deeper in the pockets while hyper-extending his elbows. He could feel the muscles in his arms tensing to their limit as his shoulders rolled back and his back straightened.

"Let's take this to the couch," Shannon said as she guided Wally to the living room where they took a seat on a plush forest green loveseat pushed against the far wall. Wally sat first, and Shannon settled close. He could feel the warmth of her thigh through their denim pants and he turned his upper body to face her. She leaned in and their mouths touched, lips slightly parted. Wally flinched and pulled away.

"It's ok. I won't bite."

Wally smiled. "I know. Just give me a minute."

He stood and Shannon nodded. "Just don't be too long."

Once Wally closed the bathroom door, he turned on the faucet and leaned over the steam rising from the bowl, arms braced on the sink edge. He looked in the mirror at his flushed face, making eye contact. He was thoughtless as he stared at himself, completely blank, just concentrating on his familiar features looking back: his thin, narrow face, rough skin, two-day-old black stubble. The mirror began to fog, starting low, creeping slowly upwards, masking his chin, then his mouth, nose and cheeks. Second by second, Wally's face was swallowed up, hidden behind the tiny beads of water adhering to the cool smooth surface. Finally, his forehead disappeared and Wally pushed back and switched off the faucet. Confident, he strode back into the living room and sat on the couch.

"Everything ok?"

Wally pressed against Shannon's body and moved in roughly for the kiss. Their lips met, and Wally felt Shannon hesitate for a second before giving in to his advances. She moaned as she leaned back, pulling Wally on top of her, grappling with his button-down shirt that was tucked into his waistband. Wally put his arm behind her back and guided her down, laying her head gently on a throw pillow behind her. Her body heaving, Wally pulled her shirt up while ducking his head down, his lips coming down on her midriff. She moaned and pulled her shirt over her head, spreading her hair across the pillow, black tangles flung out, streaming out in every direction.

Wally caressed the skin just above her hip and migrated his hand up her ribcage, cupping a breast. She continued to moan and encourage him. Suddenly, the bra was off and Wally was massaging her nipple with his thumb and forefinger, slightly pinching it as he felt it stiffen and grow hard.

Wally raised his head, moved up her body and kissed Shannon again, hard, his tongue twisting with hers as they explored each other's mouths. She let out a gasp and repositioned herself flat on her back so that they were perfectly aligned, hips to hips, body to body, face to face.

"God, you're beautiful," Wally said, suddenly overcome with a primal urge to put himself inside of her. Shannon giggled and moved her hands to Wally's collar. She beamed at him while she carefully, deliberately undid his top button and gave his shirt a slight pull. Wally felt a tug around his neck, and a flash of metal fell out of his shirt, landing with a clink on Shannon's teeth who, lips parted in a smile, was caught unprepared.

"Ah, shit!" Shannon shrieked as she struggled to sit up under Wally's body weight. "What the fuck?"

Wally pushed himself off and sat up on his knees as Shannon squirmed out from underneath him, falling to the ground between the couch and the coffee table, her hand covering her mouth.

"What, what? What is it?" Wally cried.

"My fuckin' tooth."

"What happened?"

"Something hit me."

Wally looked down at his chest and saw Julie's wedding ring that Abby had put on a chain for him. He froze as he realized it was the ring that had swung out of his shirt and hit Shannon in the tooth. He was now unsure of what to do, a feeling of dread overcoming him as he stood silently, his shirt unbuttoned and untucked, leering over her prone body, suddenly an awkward monster encroaching on foreign territory. He took a step back and slumped onto the couch. He put his face in his hands and rubbed his eyes. Shannon looked up from the floor.

"Oh, it's a ring," she said.

"I'm so sorry, I can't believe--"

"Hey, hey, it's ok," reassured Shannon. "I don't think it did any damage. Just clanged off my tooth and surprised me. I'm ok." Wally raised his head and looked at her still rubbing her mouth from her position on the floor. She was smiling though. "Really, it's ok."

Wally shook his head. "I think I should leave," he said, standing, looking around the room for his belongings.

"No, no. It doesn't have to be a deal breaker. It's kind of funny."

Wally struggled to tuck in his shirt as he stumbled for the door. "I need to-- I need to-- I should go."

The last thing he saw was Shannon shirtless, splayed out on the floor next to the couch holding her hand over her mouth, her black hair cascading off her head past her shoulders, a puzzled look on her face.

18

As a boy, it had been a mystery to Wally--a big black hole that continually spit out bowling balls. One at a time they'd come spinning back a few seconds after being hurled thirty feet down the alley, popping back up as if they'd never been thrown. Wally would sit by the hole and rise up to organize the balls as they were returned, being careful that each one rolled down the tracks on the side it had come from. He then marked the order of the various players, ensuring that their balls, the ones they had selected from the scores of racks that lined the bullpen, were waiting for them, first in line, ready to be tossed down the alley. But it was the hole itself that fascinated Wally, and he had this urge to put his hand down its gullet, past the spinning wheels to see what lurked below. It got to the point that it obsessed him and he sought out little moments when his parents' backs were turned and he could explore and probe its mouth, just to see what would happen. Would his hand be severed at the wrist? Would it pop out the far end of the machine? Would he be electrocuted? Or was there a safety mechanism that protected little boys from their curiosity? He didn't dare follow through with actually putting his hands in the hole, but he nonetheless sought out times when he could--if he wanted to--stick his hands into the dark, black hole.

"Wally, you're doing it again."

"What?" Wally rubbed his face with both hands, pushing the daydream out of his head. Abby, her long, black hair tucked into a tight ponytail, stood in front of him, her hands on her hips, imploring him to stand up.

"Your turn," she said, motioning at the glossy parquet bowling lane to her left. "We need a strike to win." Wally could see Annette and Geoff behind Abby, sitting on the hard plastic egg-shaped seats bolted to the floor, looking at him with queer looks on their faces.

"You got this, Wally?" Annette asked. She craned her neck around Abby, making sure to make eye contact with Wally as she nodded her head.

"Of course he's got this," said Geoff, encouragingly. "He knows the stakes."

Wally stood up and looked up at the video screen above their lane. SPARE US YOUR BOWLSHIT was down by twenty-two pins to THREE KNUCKLES DEEP in the tenth frame, and the last roll of the night was his. A strike would give SPARE US YOUR BOWLSHIT the win, propelling them to the league finals next week.

Wally glanced to his right at the four tech dudes who made up THREE KNUCKLES DEEP. They were wearing vintage bowling shirts with their names embroidered on the breasts--Caleb, Blake, Cole and Lil' Linus--and had various stages of facial hair, from two-day-old stubble to a full-on

Civil War general beard. They'd been drinking beer out of a pitcher all night and subsequently talking shit to Geoff, Abby, Annette and Wally across the aisle. But now they were silent, stone-faced as Wally walked past them to the ball rack.

Wally had been reluctant to join the team. Originally, Julie had been the fourth member of SPARE US YOUR BOWLSHIT and had even come up with the name. Then, several weeks after Wally had phoned Abby to tell her about his suicide attempt on the bridge, he'd gotten a call from Geoff, inviting him to join them for their weekly league games. He initially didn't think he'd like playing, but Wally quickly warmed to the outings. Standing up on the approach, Wally could focus on the ten pins standing in front of him down the lane, clearing his mind for a few seconds before he let the ball fly as hard as he could, watching the pins explode in a flurry of white and red. Wally hadn't always thrown with aggression, but the new approach seemed to work, adding dozens of pins to his average as he quickly became one of the best throwers in the league. Previously content to be merely participants, SPARE US YOUR BOWLSHIT had become a force within the league and a favorite to win the final. And, now, Wally had led them to the championship game.

Wally paused at the step up to the approach and took a deep breath. A pock-marked green rental sat next to an earth-blue polished marble ball monogramed in gold letters spelling out Lil' Linus. Wally picked up the rental, inserted his fingers into the holes and held the ball up to his chin. He was about to start his approach when a young girl in the lane adjacent jumped onto the stage next to him, throwing etiquette out the window.

"Hey--" shouted Geoff, but he was quickly interrupted by Annette.

"Let her go. It's fine," she said.

"For Christ's sake, this is a league match." Geoff argued, but Annette just shot him a look.

Wally had noticed the girl throughout the night. She was there with her family celebrating her sixth birthday surrounded by plates of snack bar nachos, small paper cups filled with soda and metallic balloons with cartoon characters imploring her to "Celebrate in Style" or "Have a Cool Day".

Wally watched wordlessly as the girl, golden curls falling gently past her shoulders over her pink tea party dress, shuffled up to the foul line next to Wally, cradling a size eight in her arms. She stopped at the line and bent over, gently placing the ball on the parquet floor. Her hair fell forward covering her face as she straddled the ball and, with all her might, pushed it down the lane. The girl quickly turned to run back to her seat next to her parents as the ball crept away from her, plopping down before turning to her mother as if in mid-conversation. Her unattended ball began to lose steam on its journey down the lane and sliced to the right. A foot before hitting the ten pin, it tipped over the rim of the lane and gently rolled into the gutter. The safety bar immediately came down and swept the untouched pins away, clearing the deck for the next player. The girl, sipping from her soda, dimples turned inward, was completely unaware of the result, uncaring and unassuming.

Wally turned his attention back to his lane as Annette, Geoff and Abby shouted encouragement from behind him. Wally peered over the top of his ball as he took a deep breath and began his run up to the throw. He took a step with his left foot first, then his right and started to bring the ball down the side of his body. His left hand came off the ball as it reached its trough down around his right butt cheek and changed direction, his right arm, grasping the ball with two fingers and his thumb flung the ball forward. The chipped green rental flew through the air a few feet and landed in the middle of the lane. It seemed to gain velocity as it spun forward until it crashed into the pins at the end of the alley. When the carnage was over, a single pin stood upright at the far left corner, the rest sprawled out in the deck and the pit, still roiling from the impact. Then, in a providence of luck, a single pin tapped against the lone holdout, causing it to teeter back and forth a few times before succumbing to physics.

"Steeeeeerrrrrrr-ike!" Geoff exclaimed from the bullpen as he pantomimed a baseball umpire calling out a batter. The tech bros groaned as Wally pivoted on his heel, pumped his fist and sauntered back across the parquet floor, a smile beaming.

Geoff, Abby and Annette met Wally in the bullpen and threw their arms around him, cheering and shouting his name. Geoff slapped Wally on the back and beamed while Abby bent over and hugged Wally around the waist, nuzzling her face in his stomach. She let out a scream that was muffled by his sweater as Annette held on to his shoulders and jumped up and down, her red hair brushing across her shoulders.

"Ok, ok. It's no big deal," Wally said, but his beaming smile betrayed his excitement. He tried to wriggle loose, but the others held on and wouldn't let him escape their grasp.

"On to the finals!" exclaimed Abby, finally letting go of Wally's midriff and throwing her hands in the air.

The normally reserved Annette pivoted to face their opponents. "Yeah, bitches! What's up now?" she screamed in their face, punctuating her question by slamming her fist in her hand. The men just waved her away and turned back to their pitcher of beer.

"Let's go celebrate," Geoff said as they started to gather their things. "First round's on me."

Several hours later, the latest finalists in the Presido Over Thirty Bowling League found themselves in Geoff's new blue convertible, the top down, music blaring. They were approaching the onramp to the Golden Gate Bridge, and it was almost midnight with the Bridge and Tunnel crowd starting their Saturday night migration back to Marin.

The quartet had celebrated their victory at a dive bar in the Marina with several pints and a round or two of house tequila shots. Wally had been reluctant to partake in the shots, but the others urged him on, reminding him that he'd been the key to their victory.

A few drinks in, Geoff had suggested they take a ride across the bridge to an overlook in Marin County that gave them a spectacular view of the Bay Area, stretching from Berkeley in the east to San Jose to the south. Abby pulled a joint out of her purse and suggested they make the view even more spectacular.

Now, with Geoff and Annette in the front seat and Wally and Abby in the back, the car rocketed across the elevated causeway past Chrissy Fields where Wally and Julie often walked Joey and collected rocks and shells for their garden. Wally had his seatbelt tightly secured around his lap and torso, and he lifted up his face as they sped down the raised highway through the old army base that guarded the entrance to the bay. The air was cool and crisp and a little wet from the sea, stinging Wally's cheeks and making him flush. His ears stung as well, and he pressed his hands that he had been warming in his jacket pocket against them until they started to get the feeling back. The orange glow of the streetlamps lining the highway streaked through his vision as he looked up, blurred by the heavy fog rolling up the coast. The noise from the wind made it impossible to hear anything said in the front seats where Geoff and Annette were content to do their own thing. Geoff, admittedly slightly buzzed, concentrated on the road while Annette stared out the window, playing DJ and singing along to her iPod.

Wally and Abby looked straight ahead as the convertible passed slower vehicles, winding up onto the trestle of the iconic bride.

"Whatcha thinking about?" Abby asked Wally. From his angle her streaming hair looked like it extended past the end of the trunk, flying freely behind Geoff's convertible like streamers on a ten-year-old girl's bicycle.

"This is where I almost jumped." He turned his hands over and over in his lap, his fingers intertwining and untwining. His hands were cold from the roaring wind, and he could feel them being warmed by the heat emanating from his crotch.

"Oh, right." Abby leaned forward, placing her hand gently on Wally's shoulder. He sighed, finally looking up. Abby was looking at him, peering almost. Wally smiled. "Do you want to talk about it?" she asked.

Wally shook his head and Abby took her hand off his

shoulder. "Not really," he responded. Then added, "Maybe some day."

"Ok then," she said as she nodded. "Tell me one thing about Julie that I don't know."

Wally chuckled and paused in thought. "There's a lot you don't know." They sat in silence as the car traversed the main span, Wally holding his breath, not daring to breathe until they landed safely on the Marin side of the Golden Gate. Wally sighed, then said, "Julie was a car thief."

Abby snorted. "Go on."

"As you know, we didn't use her car much in the city, but we used to drive around Antioch when we'd visit Bonnie and Nate."

"Ok," Abby said, elongating her vowels, anticipating the punchline. She looked at Wally and smiled, teeth showing through chapped lips. Her cheeks were flushed as well, though Wally remembered they'd been red in the bar, likely due to alcohol rather than the stinging wind.

"We used to take BART out to the East Bay and stay the night a few times a year. Easter. Thanksgiving. If they were driving us to the airport the next day. Times like that. Her parents go to bed kind of early--"

"--how early?"

"I don't know. Nine o'clock? Nine thirty? It was always early."

Wally paused and looked up to gauge Abby's interest, and she motioned for him to continue.

"So, we'd watch some TV, do some reading. Julie would play around on this ukulele that she'd had as a kid. But eventually we'd get bored."

"Uh, oh," Abby said. "It gets dangerous whenever Julie

gets bored."

Wally smiled and continued, "It wasn't that bad. Julie would take the keys to her parents' Miata and we'd push the car in neutral down the driveway. I'd jump in right when she turned the ignition, and she'd peel out down the little country road where she'd grown up. We'd crank up the radio and sing along. I'd tease her that in twenty years we'd hear Sunset Revolution songs on classic rock stations. Mainly we'd just drive and drive, chatting about the strangest things. It was weird because we'd talk about things we'd never bring up with each other in the city. It was as if the car, stolen from her parents' garage, was this bubble where we were safe from judgments. And those truly were the best conversations. We'd rarely bring them up with each other later, but I'll never forget them."

"What did you talk about?"

"Nah. Those things are just for me."

Abby nodded as if she understood.

"Ok. How long were these rides?" Abby asked as Geoff accelerated up the windy highway through the hills overlooking Fort Baker and Alcatraz in the distance.

"Oh, hours, it seemed," Wally continued. "We'd drive around this little town in the Delta where she grew up, and where she became the person I fell in love with. There are all these dead ends that run right up and into all these canals in the delta, so it was impossible to tell exactly where you were going. Julie claimed that everyone in town navigated by the two main landmarks in town, the hospital and the federal prison."

"Yeah, she used to tell me that as well. Seemed to be a point of pride."

"Well, both were lit up real bright with huge spotlights filling the night air. Didn't seem like reliable guides to me, though, because inevitably we'd get lost every time."

Wally stopped and pondered what he'd just said. "She'd get lost in her own hometown--a little suburb of about six thousand people. But that was Jules. Her own weird little person."

"Yeah, she was weird," Abby agreed.

The car sped into Robin Williams tunnel, and the sound of car horns echoed off the ceramic tile walls, exponentially increasing in volume. Wally and Abby put their hands over their ears, but Geoff, in the front seat, didn't seem to mind and even let out a few beeps of his own. Annette flashed him a look as they exited out of the tunnel and back into the cool Marin night. The highway pointed downhill, and lights from Sausalito appeared over the crest of the hill, twinkling in the far off distance.

After it quieted down, Wally turned to Abby. "Ok, my turn. What do you think was the weirdest thing about Julie?" he asked.

"You ever been to Nara Sushi?"

Wally shook his head.

"Really? It's on Polk Street, right by your apartment."

"Yeah, I know the place, but I don't think I ever went inside."

"Ok. Yeah. Well, I guess it was our place then. Julie and I used to go there together, and we'd sit at the bar and compliment the sushi chefs on their knife skills. I'd always try to get her to share some rolls but Julie always insisted on ordering her own. It was always spicy tuna, and she wouldn't let me have any."

Wally snorted. "Sounds like Julie. She used to do the same thing when we'd get tapas." He knew that Julie was particular about her food and rarely shared. "It was an odd trait, right? Especially for someone as kind and generous as Julie was in other areas of her life."

"Yes, totally," Abby continued. "I never understood her thing about sharing food. Nearly every other decision she made was so considerate. I'd ask her what movie we should watch, and she'd inevitably pick one that she knew I wanted to see. Where should we hang out? Again, she'd suggest someplace convenient for me--"

"Except food," Wally interrupted.

"Yeah, totally. She wanted what she wanted. She didn't share--"

"And, if you had a problem with that, she didn't give a fuck."

"Once I stole a fry off her plate, and she pushed it across the table and made the waitress get her another order," Abby said.

"I thought I'd be romantic one Valentine's Day and pre-order a bowl of mussels at a place in Fisherman's Wharf for us to share. She made me eat the whole thing while she munched on a salad."

"She once stabbed me with her fork."

They erupted in laughter, together, as Geoff drove down US-101 through Mill Valley. Abby turned to him, and Wally saw that her eyes were bloodshot and her nose was running. More tears came and he reached over and took Abby's hand in his, clasped it down over the red leather bench seat between them. He pressed firmly, giving her a slight squeeze, and her thumb reached up to stroke his palm.

19

Compulsion drove him to pick at the small, hard scab on his wrist, his nails catching the edge of the dried crust, separating it from the new skin underneath. A drop of blood formed and slowly streaked the underside of his forearm, pooling at the base. Wally continued to scratch, and the stream grew thicker and redder. In one motion, the entire scab came off, exposing a vein, blood now spouting in the air, splattering his hand, torso and legs then his face. Wally plunged his wrist in the tub, under the water line, watching the red clouds expand in the bath, waiting for the end.

The buzzer sounded, and Joey bounded out of Wally's lap on the couch. The Jack Russell skidded across the hardwood floor as he lunged toward the door, the poor traction causing him to hover and sprint in mid-air like the Wile E. Coyote in the old Warner Brothers cartoons. Wally threw off the throw and swung his legs around. His feet planted firmly on the floor, he stood and slowly made his way to the front door, deliberately taking his time as Joey scratched at the crack.

"Hello?" Wally said into the intercom.

"It's me."

Joey barked in response, unable to handle the unexpected activity. Wally pressed the button to unlock the main door downstairs, and he heard the it unlatch, swing open and slam shut. Wally opened the door of his apartment and heard footsteps echo up the stairway and down the hall. Joey squeezed through Wally's legs and ran to the top of the stairs, head up, ears perked, tail wagging back and forth.

"Joey! Hey buddy," came a woman's voice from a flight down. "I hear your panting. I'm coming mister!"

A moment later Wally saw Joey crane his neck forward toward an outstretched palm a few steps below his snout. The hand moved up to stroke the dog on the top of his head between his ears. The woman then stepped up onto the landing and came down the hall with Joey close on her heels.

"Walter-ini!" exclaimed Abby. She stumbled toward Wally with her hands extended out to her sides, palming the walls for support as she walked. Her hair was mussed and her jacket mis-buttoned, the right side an inch or two higher than her left. A scarf was wrapped haphazardly around her neck with one of its ends dragging behind her, brushing up against the heels of her sneakers as she walked. Joey nipped at the cuff of her jeans and the end of the scarf, his ears still on full alert, his tail continuing to wag.

Abby stumbled forward and fell into Wally's arms, her face buried in his chest. Wally caught her under her arms and dragged her into the apartment. She regained her footing as they entered the living room and smacked her lips.

"You're drunk."

Abby laughed. "Of course I am. I had some drinks after work," she slurred. She was standing on her own but her body was swaying and one eye was inexplicably closed. She stuck out her tongue and pointed it up at her nose.

"Sounds like you had more than just a couple of drinks," Wally responded as he shut the door after Joey.

The dog went straight to Abby and began sniffing her from the knees down from every angle. Abby looked, and upon seeing the dog again, let out a playful yelp. She stretched out her arms and tried to bend down but her equilibrium failed her and she fell backwards against the wall, sliding to the floor. Joey saw this as an invitation and started to paw at her body. Abby squealed again and pulled the dog in close, cuddling him against her face.

"Oh, you're so cute," she cooed, then hiccupped.

Joey was happy to oblige and started licking her face. Then his pink lipstick made an appearance and his back legs started to move back and forth against Abby's leg.

"Uh... you may want to stop him," Wally blurted, but it was too late. Joey was in full hump mode, rubbing his penis against Abby, drooling, tongue hanging out, a sly doggie grin on his snout.

"Oh boy," Abby said as the realization of what Joey was doing to her hit. "Get him off. Get him off."

Wally bent down to push Joey off, but Abby's squirming on the floor got her legs tangled with his. Wally tried to straighten up and balance himself against the wall, but Abby reached up and clumsily pulled him down. All three collapsed in a heap, limbs and scarf tangled. Abby tried to rise, but her elbow caught Wally in the ribs. He cried out and had to stop supporting his weight, sending him crashing back on top of her. Meanwhile Joey kept humping whatever he found underneath him--Abby, Wally, the scarf.

"Wait, wait. Stop squirming," Wally cried out. "Get your elbow off and stop pushing me."

Abby didn't hear him, her senses seemingly dulled by the alcohol and an overwhelming desire to right herself by any means necessary. She continued to struggle and poke and prod Wally as he tried to separate himself from the pile. After Abby finally stopped struggling, Wally found himself underneath her body, face to face, her scarf wrapped around both of them, pressing their torsos together tightly. Wally paused at the absurdity of it all and forcibly shooed the dog away with his free leg. Seemingly getting the hint, Joey slunk off to the other room, and Abby looked up.

"Was it good for you?" Wally teased.

Abby laughed. "Oh. My. God. Your dog is such a hornball."

"Hornball? Did you just say hornball?"

"Yes. Yes I did." She hiccupped.

"What's up with your scarf? This thing is a death trap. Besides, it's sixty degrees out there. Who needs a scarf?"

"The fog's coming in."

Abby's face softened as the two locked eyes.

"Uh... yeah. It's getting nippy out there," stammered Wally.

"Did you just say nipply?"

Wally nervously laughed. "I most certainly did not. I think you heard what you wanted to hear."

"Shut up."

The two paused again, Abby's lips hovering just over

Wally's mouth. Suddenly, Abby sucked in and pulled Wally's head closer. Their lips met, his plump and moisturized, Abby's chapped and chafed from an afternoon of drinking. Lost in the moment, Wally let himself be taken in for a second, then pulled away, just in time to see her eyes slowly open and her smile fade.

"What the fuck was that?" he demanded as a tinge of panic crept up from his stomach. He sat up and pushed himself back against the hallway's opposite wall as far as he could get.

"Oh, god. I'm sorry. I shouldn't have done that."

"No. No you shouldn't have. What are you even doing here?"

Abby remained motionless, still splayed out on the floor, looking up at the ceiling, her eyes misting. "I--I needed to talk to you."

"Is that a good idea? You're drunk."

"I needed the courage."

"The courage for what?"

"To tell you what I came here to tell you."

"And what's that?" He not so much said it as spit the words at her.

Abby rolled over on her side and propped herself up on her elbow. She struggled to sit up, and finally managed to get her back up against the front door, facing Wally across the hall. Their legs were next to each other, parallel, two tracks going in opposite directions.

"The other night after bowling, in Geoff's car."

"Yes?"

Abby broke eye contact. "I miss Julie," she said, and the tears started streaming down her face.

"Oh boy. Don't cry. I hate it when women cry." Abby laughed but the tears kept coming. Her face scrunched around her nose, and she wiped her nose with her sleeve. "We all miss her, believe me."

Abby nodded. "I miss her so much, and I just want to follow through on her request to make you happy."

"Make me happy? What are you talking about? What request?"

Abby looked up and locked eyes with Wally. "Julie wanted us to end up together if anything happened to her."

The air went out of Wally's lungs, and he could feel his face getting warm. He struggled to get up, but Abby reached across the hall and latched onto his arm. He wriggled free and stood, towering over Abby, hands on his hips, lips tightly pursed, teeth grinding.

"We were talking a few days before she died around the time of Geoff and Annete's party. Potey was there, too.

"Potey?"

"Well, he was there, but I don't think he was listening. I guess it doesn't matter."

"Julie was talking about this with Potey?"

"He was just there. He wasn't even worth mentioning. He was just being Potey."

"So, what? We're supposed to get together now? Should we start dating? Start off with something small like bowling and then graduate to dinner and eventually you were going to trick me all the way to the alter? Was Potey going to officiate?"

"Stop. It's not like that. I didn't take it seriously until we had that moment on the bridge in Geoff's car. I felt a connection and thought, hell, why not give it a try."

"Yeah, why not give it a try?" he mimicked, throwing up his arms over his hunched shoulders. "What the hell, Wally will be up for it." He paused, looked down at Abby, her eyes red and teary, and said cooly, "It's been less than a year. Julie's body isn't even cold yet and you're here hitting on me."

Now it was Abby who grew visibly angry. "Come on. You know that's not how this went down. Besides, aren't you being a little hypocritical?"

Wally frowned and shot her a look.

"You're very neurotic," Abby declared.

"That's your explanation? I'm neurotic?"

"Yes-- sort of-- I guess. Look, you're neurotic, but Julie was just as neurotic as you are. She was scared to death about leaving you behind with no one to take care of you. She did you know--take care of you."

"I know."

"Well, she was scared about what would happen to you if she left. It made her sick, but unlike you, she internalized it."

Wally breathed deep, not quite a sigh, but a tired little exhale.

"Do you remember a gig that Julie and the band did last Spring up in Sonora? It was some tiny music festival, and the band was playing on a Sunday. You didn't make the trip because you had to work the next day."

Wally nodded.

"Well, you were home all day, and you could have done anything you wanted. Hung out with friends, seen a movie, gone on a hike. Anything you wanted. The day was yours. Do you remember what you did?"

Wally shook his head.

"You stayed home and made Julie lunch for the next day.

And not just a turkey sandwich. You made her ramen. Authentic ramen. You knew that she'd be getting in around noon after spending the night out in the mountains, and you wanted her to have something nice to eat. You grilled a pork tenderloin and sliced it real thin like she liked it. I think you even boiled an egg and chopped up something like four different types of vegetables. You then left out a package of Ramen and instructions for her about how to put it all together. It must have taken you like three hours."

Wally only vaguely remembered this scenario, but it sounded like something he would have done. He scanned his memory for a clue as to what was different about that particular time but came up empty. In fact, he didn't even think that he or Julie had addressed it when he came home from work later that afternoon. It all seemed so, so mundane.

"That scared her to death, Wally," Abby continued. "It really did."

"What do you mean?"

"She couldn't fathom how someone like you could love her unconditionally like you did. And you made no qualms about showing her that love through these little gestures. That commitment, that passion, that scared her."

"I don't understand. Didn't she love me back?"

Abby jumped to her feet and slammed her palm against the wall, inches from Wally's face.

"Damnit! Yes!" She shouted. "And that scared her most of all. She couldn't believe how much she loved you. I mean, fuck, you loved her so much you made plans for her for when you'd no longer be in her life. You'd still be doing these little gestures and taking care of her from the grave. It could be years later, and she'd get some care package in the mail from you. Do you know how fucked up that would make someone? She'd never be able to live her life. It would just be the life that you set up for her."

Wally bowed his head.

Abby paused, the palm of her hand still pressed against the wall. Her eyes were narrowed and her brow furrowed. Tears were streaming down her cheeks, and she used her sleeve to smear them across her face.

"Listen, I don't need this right now, so--"

"I'm sorry I'm not doing a good job of communicating my thoughts," she continued. "But I've had some drinks." She was visibly shaking now.

"Yeah, maybe I need a drink or two."

"Great. Let's head over to Zeki's--"

"No. I want to go alone. Stay here and keep Joey company. He seems more open to your advances."

Wally picked up his wallet and cellphone that were sitting on a table in the entryway. He shoved them in his jacket pocket and took a step forward, reaching for the doorknob behind Abby's head. She shifted her weight to the side and slid down the wall until she was slumped on the floor, back against the wall. Wally walked past without a word, leaving Abby listening to his footsteps echo down the hallway, Joey peering at her lustily from the bedroom.

20

Wally tossed a pair of athletic socks in the washer and watched them soak into the tub on top of T-shirts, soiled underpants and stinky gym shorts. The socks' navy blue material sunk under the cascade of water filling the tub, lost in a swirl of reds and greens, greys and blacks. He peered over the edge into the machine, and suddenly he grew dizzy and found himself tumbling over and over with the laundry, caught in the perpetual motion of crashing waves, their sound deafening. He lost track of up and down, left and right. He kept tossing and turning, pulled under by the force of the waves, gasping, grasping for breath, wondering if he'd ever taste air again.

A chirp woke him up. Wally opened his eyes, blinked a few times and focused on a tropical bird perched on his bedpost. It was all yellow, save for a few black streaks on its wings and a bright red bill. With Wally stirring, the bird chirped again, cocking its head to the side as if saying "Good Morning." The sound of a crashing wave came washing into the room and Wally rose and walked across the room. The bird took flight, did a lap around the four-poster bed, and Wally watched as it flew out of the building, up and over the shoreline until it disappeared from sight.

Wally wiped the sleep from his eyes and faced the warm morning sun that shone through the branches and leaves that served as the cover for the entire front side of the house that Wally was renting for the week. It was a palapa, a three-sided building on the shore, the open side facing the water where the Pacific Ocean crashed into the rainforest just south of Puerto Vallarta. Wally was on the second floor, up in the trees, and a fine mist made its way into his room, giving the furniture a nice sheen in the early morning light.

He stretched his arms over his head and walked barefoot and bare-assed across the exposed room. He stopped at the small fridge that had to be hand-cranked once every twelve hours, stooping to take out a carton of papaya juice he'd procured the night before at a small, family-run market--the only store in town. Drinking straight from the container, Wally gulped the thick, syrupy juice, a few rivulets forming in the corners of his mouth, running through his chin hairs like a slalom skier smoothly gliding through red and blue gates. He took a deep breath and burped, a sickly, sweet vapor wafting across his face.

Wally'd been in Yelapa, which was accessible only by water taxi, for two days. And why not? He needed a break from the constant reminders of Julie, her things in the closet, her scent in the bathroom, the hundreds and hundreds of things--things!--that prompted ever-distant memories of the love of his life. Besides, it was Mexico. It was warm and cheap, and he could work on his tan.

The road--a goat path, really--pulled up sharply as it passed Wally's palapa, arching up and over the rocky coastline toward what passed as town. With the ocean on his left and the outskirts of civilization on his right, Wally made his way out the front gate, down three stone steps, past a beached kayak on the shore and toward a cluster of adobe and concrete buildings huddled on the edge of the rainforest, overlooking a beautiful turquoise bay. He wore a pair of navy board shorts, a tattered yellow T-shirt and old flip flops. Crooked on his elbow was a beach bag with a towel, sunscreen and a dog-eared paperback of a Steven King novel he'd found on a shelf in his room. He deftly moved the bag from his right arm to his left as he scrambled over rock outcroppings, keeping sure to maintain balance as the path skirted the narrow patch of land between the sandy beach and the overgrown forest.

The path started to smooth out and straighten as he neared town, the tourist palapas giving way to the mix of ramshackle huts and adobe bunkers that the locals called home. Loud merengue music emanated from one of the homes, and Wally caught a glimpse through the slats in the wall of an aged woman with native features hunched over a small table, kneading dough, several small children at her feet playing with marbles, hot wheels and other assorted plastic toys. Large palm fronds grew out of the edge of the forest, casting long shadows in the morning sun where feral dogs lounged on the street, heads down, tails swishing off the flies, eyes watching Wally warily as he approached, passed and went on his way. He neared the market where he'd bought the juice, waving to the elderly proprietor through the open doors, a curious and toothless smile the only return.

The path cut past the only discernable restaurant in town, a collection of plastic tables and chairs arranged half-heartedly in a small cordoned-off courtyard, a wooden sign with a red chicken painted on its side the only indication it was a public eating place. Wally had had an early dinner there his first night here. It was a decent meal, but the place had been empty save for a few other tourists.

The next day he ran into a group of three Canadian expats who were spending a few months in town and inquired where everyone was eating.

"Be patient," one said, a tiny, rubber-banded ponytail peeking out the back of his blue mesh baseball cap. His face was weathered and wrinkled but relaxed. "The food will come to you." The other two giggled and went on their way, heading up the hillside into the rainforest as Wally shrugged and headed down toward the beach.

Sure enough, that night Wally lingered outside the market past sunset and watched the village transform from hot, dusty deserted hole-in-the-wall to a lively, energetic town, its inhabitants creeping out of the cool shadows in their homes, the humid jungle air finally cooled by the evening breeze. Christmas tree lights strung up on adobe walls transformed dusty courtyards into dance floors and eating halls. Some men lounged on beach chairs set out in the middle of the streets, and others kicked off an impromptu game of dominoes. Children chased dogs from alleyway to alleyway. Barbecues were set up, and ridiculously rich smells wafted out over the town. A man with dark features and a sunny disposition approached Wally, inviting him to take a seat at his family's table.

"Uno taco, uno dolar," he said through smiling teeth, waving in the direction of his patio. As Wally was about to nod and let himself be led into the man's home, another local came up, this one dressed a bit nicer in khaki shorts and a blue polo shirt, imploring Wally to follow him. "My wife cook better." He smiled and pointed at the first man, giving him a thumbs down. The other guy shrugged his shoulders, nodded in ascension, perhaps acquiescing that yes, the other man's wife was indeed a more accomplished cook. Wally appreciated honesty, but he went with the better food.

The man's wife greeted Wally as they entered the courtyard, motioning him to take a seat in a white plastic chair in the middle of the space. Two children, naked from the waist up, carried a folding table from inside the hut and placed it in front of him, and a third came out of the doorway with plastic forks and knives and a stack of paper napkins. The man joined Wally and implored him to choose the meat for the evening. The children leaned forward in anticipation as Wally, not wanting to be presumptuous, contemplated the possible choices.

"Carnitas?" he shrugged. Like modern-day Pancho Villas the children yelped with joy and ran into the house, chattering excitedly, pushing each other, their lanky, browned limbs tangling in the narrow doorway.

"Last turisto pick pescado," their father explained,

flashing the thumbs-down sign once again. He smiled a toothy smile, his tongue flicking behind several gaps.

Wally had bought a six-pack of beer at the market, and he pulled two out, twisting the caps off while handing one to the man. They tapped the long necks together in an audible clink and tipped them back.

The next morning, the street in front of the adobe house of the man from whom Wally got dinner the night before was deserted except for the requisite stray dog. The shutters were closed tightly save for the top slat that was pushed out, an improvement that Wally presumed helped keep in the cool night air while filtering out the heat. The sight of the home caused the sensory memories to flood his brain: richly-flavored pinto beans on top of smoked pork, a shred of cabbage and a few sprigs of fennel all wrapped up in a soft corn tortilla. His hosts kept filling his plate, and he happily complied, gorging himself on half a dozen tacos and mounds of perfectly-cooked, moist rice. He and the man easily finished off the six pack and a bottle of tequila was procured. It, too, was drained.

But now, the plastic seats and table were propped up against a wall, and there was really no evidence of the raucous evening they'd all had just a few hours before. It was as if the place had simply moved on, stripped bare and put into hibernation, but probably ready to spring to life again when the sun went down. He didn't even know his host's name, let alone anything of his past, but it didn't seem to matter. They had shared a meal, some pleasantries and a lot of booze and then went on their separate ways in this big, small modern world.

Wally dropped his bag on a beach chair at the end of a long row of seats with umbrellas interspersed, shielding a few dozen tourists from the Mexican sun. He pulled his T-shirt over his head, revealing his naked, pale torso. It was the first time he'd made it to the beach despite being in town for several days, and his complexion was baby-like, virgin skin, white as toothpaste, blue veins visible under the translucent covering. The chain that Abby had given him hung from his neck, Julie's wedding ring tangling in his sparse, stringy chest hair. Wally took a seat, leaned back and gazed past the sheltered bay that protected Yelapa from the ocean, white caps visible on the horizon. A shadow crossed his face as a young man, dark skin, dark hair, muscular frame, appeared at Wally's side. He was wearing a green polo shirt, white shorts and no shoes.

"Hola amigo," the man said, standing straight, arms behind his back. "What can I get for you?" His English was perfect without a hint of an accent.

Wally squinted into the morning sun creeping over the treetops behind him. The man smiled patiently and maintained eye contact as Wally sat up.

"Is it too early for shots?"

The man laughed, relaxing his rigid stance. "Maybe amigo. It depends on your constitution."

Wally grinned back. Perhaps a shot was too much this early.

"I have the thing for you, amigo."

The man turned and headed toward the thatched hut at the edge of the beach that served as a cafe. Rather than take his place behind the bar, the man surprised Wally by continuing past the hut and disappearing into the rainforest. An image of the man showing up with fermented goats' milk or some sort of scorpion cocktail flashed through Wally's mind.

Suddenly a head popped up above the thick canopy of foliage, and Wally recognized the man's muscular frame shimmying up a tall, thin palm tree at the edge of the forest. The long trunk curved as it cleared the lower brush, and soon the man was sitting upright, straddling the trunk, using his massive forearms to inch his way upward. Wally watched as he reached the lowest branches and pulled a giant machete out of the waistband of his shorts. The man cut the blade in a single downward motion, sending three coconuts to the ground. Calmly, he then sheathed the machete, swung his legs up on the trunk behind him, and now laying on his stomach, started to slide down the tree. In a few seconds he disappeared into the bush.

The man emerged from the jungle holding the coconuts, carrying them into the thatched bar. Still twisted in his chair, Wally watched the man peel off and discard the exocarp and slice off the top of the fruit with the machete. He then collected a variety of liquors from behind the bar and poured generous amounts of each directly into the mouth of the coconut. Clear liquor was mixed with dark liquor, long pours with short splashes. Done with the liquors, the man then opened what looked like a six-ounce juice can and poured half of its contents into the drink. He then inserted a long straw, and with drink in tow, started to make its way across the sand toward Wally.

Wally was transfixed, amazed and impressed really, that this strange mixture was on its way toward him on a brown plastic servers' tray.

"Hola, amigo," the man said as he approached. "Just the thing for you this morning."

"Looks strong," Wally responded, his eyes growing bigger the closer the coconut came. The man put it down on a table next to Wally's chair.

"No worries, amigo. It's just fruit juice. All natural."

They both laughed at the obvious lie as Wally picked up the coconut and was surprised to find that the exposed husk was soft, almost like horsehair. He peered into the hole that was cut into the top, moving the container around, sloshing the mixture inside. Wally could see bits of coconut floating on top of a light beige color--a hue he recognized from grade school when he would mix every paint in the spectrum. Closing his eyes, he placed his lips around the tip of the straw and sucked. Sweet liquid siphoned into his mouth, and he swished it around with his tongue. He expected the drink to be thick or syrupy like rum, but it was watery, surprisingly refreshing, albeit with a bit of a kick.

Wally opened his eyes and beamed up at the man above him who continued to smile, seemingly anticipating the gringo's reaction.

"Delicious."

The man's smile transformed into a grin. "We call it a choco-loco. It's perfect after a night of drinking."

Wally nodded and took another sip. This time, a chunk of

coconut made its way up the straw, adding a bit of texture to the liquid. He chewed the pulp and swallowed. "We call it hair of the dog in the states."

The man turned and spoke over his shoulder as he headed to another group of tourists on the far side of the bar. "My name is Sebastian," he said. "I doubt you'll be needing anything else the rest of the morning, but if you do, let me know."

Wally giggled, a strange feeling rising from his stomach into his chest, the idea of drinking liquor so early in the morning emboldening him. He rested the coconut on his chest, placing it against the ring on his chain as he sprawled out on the beach chair, the end of the straw settling on the middle of his chin. Yes, he thought, this is going to be an interesting day.

A few hours later, properly hydrated, Wally felt the urge to relieve himself. He sat up and glanced around for the facilities. Sebastian happened to be walking by, a tray of drinks in his hands, and Wally called out to him.

"Banos?"

Sebastian grinned and stopped.

"You have two options, amigo." He nodded first at the ocean and then back at the rainforest. "Take your pick."

Wally laughed. Right, right. Emboldened by the booze, Wally swung his legs to the side of his beach chair and pressed his fists into the cushion next to him, lifting himself a few inches with his hand, and then he let his legs do the rest of the work. Upon standing, his head immediately began to swoon, and he lost his balance. Wally reached for the umbrella to catch himself, but being anchored in sand, it wasn't much help as a stabilizing force. He felt himself falling forward, face first in the canvas shield, but managed to take a quick half-step to maintain control of his body. Somewhat stabilized, balancing on the balls of his feet in the sand, knees bent, one foot slightly in front of the other, arms outstretched with his palms down, Wally took a step toward the water. A wave crashed into the shore, white water cascading up the a steep slope of the beach, petering out just before it reached his toes. Wally took another step, and another wave crashed onto shore, this one a bit bigger and louder. Off to his side a water taxi from Puerta Vallarta pulled up to the beach, and several servers, Sebastian among them, waded into the surf toward the boat. The bow rose up and down as each wave came crashing in, and the taxi driver started tossing suitcases over the railing at the waiters in thigh-deep water. They caught the suitcases one at a time and passed them, fireman chain like, up onto the beach. On the far side of the boat, about a dozen or so tourists, their sea legs disappearing as fast as they'd gained them, scrambled over a railing and dropped into the surf. Then it was a race to higher, drier ground as oncoming waves chased them onshore.

Wally giggled at the absurdity of it all, and, thinking there had to be a safer pissing, he turned his back to the sea, bent down to pick up his flipflops and stumbled headlong into the bush. Wally pushed aside large palm fronds in his way as he went further into the forest. He soon came across a few low buildings made of sheets of corrugated steel, fastened at the corners by heavy wires punched through holes in the metal. Chicken wire ran everywhere, as patches of brush had been cleared for poultry, a few goats and other livestock. The compound was just a few steps into the forest but completely hidden from the tourists on the beach who were happily and obliviously sipping their margaritas, pina coladas and cervezas.

Wally continued past the buildings, nodding to a scrawny goat that was quietly munching on a small patch of grass in its paddock. He then came to a dirt path that led further into the forest. Curious, Wally tossed his flipflops onto the ground and eased his feet into the plastic handles, securing the thin layer of rubber to his soles. Following the path, Wally continued into the forest, the brush around him growing thicker with each step he took along the dusty trail. He came to a fork that had a sign pointing in opposite directions. Despite the fact that the only Spanish he knew came from an Offspring song, Wally had no problem translating the words. Cascada pointed to the left and Pueblo pointed to the right.

The urge to pee hadn't gone away, but the bush was too thick to step off the trail and he certainly wasn't going to risk stepping on a poisonous snake, man-eating lizard or whatever dangers that lurked in the underbrush. But he certainly wasn't going to relieve himself in the middle of the path either. For all he knew, this could be main street and a gaggle of school kids could come around the bend at any second.

Driven forward by the choco-loco putting pressure on his courage and on his bladder, Wally turned left and headed deeper into the forest. The path followed a wide creek bed that had a small trickle running down the middle. There was at least twenty feet of rough, pebbly sand on either side of the banks before the bush closed in. The bed was strewn with plastic bags, old bicycle parts, broken appliances and other junk that must have been carried downstream when the river's flow was much stronger. It was dry season, Wally remembered, and the waterline was no doubt much higher at other times of the year. There were more buildings on the other side of the creek bed held together by concrete blocks, sheets of metal and wire. Blue tarps covered the seams, flapping noisily in the wind.

As the path continued, it sloped up, gaining elevation, and Wally had to climb over large rocks and boulders that lay in his way. His flipflops got caught in rocky crags as he continued, causing him to stumble as the sun beat down through the opening made in the canopy by the path. The temperature was ten to fifteen degrees warmer than on the beach and it was much more humid, causing beads of sweat to form on Wally's face, neck and back.

It had been at least fifteen minutes, and Wally hadn't seen a single person. It was time. Wally unzipped his pants and aimed at a particularly large frond three feet off the trail, splattering it with a heavy stream of dark yellow piss. His urine smelled sweet, and it was a little cloudy. Wally felt good, the tension melting off his body as he emptied his bladder.

Wally continued the scramble up the rocks, and after a few minutes crested the hill, coming to a concrete building just off the path. Large and colorful advertising covered the entire front side except for a narrow door. This was open, but the bright light outside was unable to penetrate more than a foot or two into the building. The low hum of a generator combined with the advertising told Wally that this was a market, similar to the one he'd frequented in town.

Wally stepped through the entrance and stood there, letting his eyes adjust to the dim light. While momentarily blinded, he could see the faint glow of a television set on a counter to his right and hear the rat-tat-tat of fast-speaking Spanish coming from its speakers. The sweet smell of plantains was strong all around him, and eventually he saw a shelf in front of him covered by the fragrant fruit start to come into focus.

"Hola."

Wally spun at the direction of the voice and saw a small aged man with a brown, creased face sitting behind the counter, facing the television. He was wearing a flannel, long-sleeved shirt and a pale cowboy hat with leather trim. The man smiled and gestured with open arms at the goods in his store, seemingly inviting Wally to browse the shelves and purchase something. Wally nodded and stepped toward a cooler at the far end of the room. He opened its door and took a small bottle of water off the shelf. Despite being refrigerated the drink was cool but not cold. At the counter, the man took Wally's paper pesos and made change with coins.

"Choco-loco?" the man asked, thrusting his chin in Wally's direction, a slight smile on his face.

Surprised, Wally nodded.

The man laughed and plugged his nose with his thumb and forefinger and waved his other hand in front of his face as if warding off a bad smell.

"I smell like booze, huh?"

The man nodded and broke into a hearty chuckle. Wally laughed back, surprisingly proud that he smelled like liquor so early in the morning. He was on vacation, trying to get his life back together, and everyone needed to smell like booze once in a while.

Wally shrugged his shoulders. "I need a shower, perhaps." The man's laughter petered out, replaced by a confused look. Wally pantomimed rubbing soap under his armpits, but the man still looked lost. "Cascada."

"Ah, Cascada." The man nodded as his eyes twinkled from the light emanating off his TV. They were cloudy blue.

"Cascada bueno?"

"Si, si. Bueno cascada." The man held up one finger. "Una milla." He pointed over his shoulder in the direction Wally had been walking.

"Gracias," Wally responded. He picked up his water bottle, unscrewed the cap and took a giant swallow. The liquid was room temperature but Wally didn't care. It was wet. It was refreshing. It was exciting.

Wally stripped off his board shorts and T-shirt and waded into the clear fresh water, surrounded by slick, moss-covered boulders at the base of a tall, cascading waterfall. The crystal-clear water in the small pool came half-way up Wally's thighs, just short of his crotch. Sunlight streamed through the water, letting Wally see the mossy rocks at the bottom of the pool. Small fish no bigger than his pinky darted in and out of the dark crevices, nibbling at the skin on his feet and legs. Wally waded toward the far side of the pool where a cascade of water fell twenty feet into the water, splashing several feet in every direction, churning the calm surface. Looking skyward at the source of the water, Wally noticed ferns growing out of cracks in the soaked cliff face, and that the stone was covered with green lichen. Large, dark flies buzzed through the air, collecting moisture on their wings as the mist blew up and out from the falls.

Wally reached the waterfall and ducked his head into the cascading water, placing his outstretched palms against the slippery cliff face. The water beat down on the back of his head and neck, aggressively kneading his tense muscles. Keeping contact with the cliff, Wally pulled his head out of the water, took a deep breath and plunged it back in. The pounding water was relentless, and the chain around his neck was pushed and pulled in several directions as the water splashed up and around his chest. This time, Wally stayed under longer than before, then, after taking another breath, stuck his head under the spout again. The third time he let go of the cliff face and sank to his knees. The round, worn rocks scraped the skin on his shins. He lowered his head so his face was underwater with the waterfall continuing to pound the back of head. A minute passed, and Wally held steady, acutely self-aware of his place in the universe. Time seemed to stop as his life with Julie played out in his mind. His chance discovery of her band at Hemlock Tavern. Introducing himself and buying her that first beer. The first several months of dating when he doted on her while she showed disinterest. Wearing her down, falling in love, moving in together and finally tying the knot, legally and symbolically bonding them together forever. The fact that she was out of his league as a lover and as a person haunting him throughout their relationship. Hating himself for being neurotic but helpless to stop his destructive behavior. Sad that he would never again be able to tell her that he loved her.

Wally's lungs burned, but he kept his head down,

focusing on the steady beat upon the nape of his neck. His ears lay half in and half out of the water, the surface of the pool ebbing and flowing into his canals, alternatively blocking the crash of the falls and muffling it from underwater. He seemed to slip in and out of awareness as well, the calmness of his being swallowed up by oxygen-deprived pure sorrow and pain before returning to peace yet again. On and on the pattern repeated in Wally's mind as the water pounded the back of his head, his lungs ready to burst, his heart ready to explode.

Abruptly, Wally straightened up, drawing breath as his face broke free of the pool's surface, taking deep gasps as he fell over backward away from the falling water, the mossy, lichen-covered rock face and his demons. Wally staggered on the smooth rocks under the surface but caught himself before his head become submerged once again. He turned over on his hands and knees and with the water up to his chin he willed himself to crawl through the shallow water toward the bank, dragging his beleaguered, naked body behind him. Exhausted and out of breath, he collapsed on the outcropping where he'd entered the pool, draping the top half of his body over the rock next to his flipflops, pile of clothes and empty water bottle. His lungs heaved, trying to catch his breath. After what seemed like many minutes, Wally pulled the rest of his body out of the water and lay on his back, face toward the sky, his naked body splayed out in the open. The sun beat down on his wet skin, the water beading and slowly dripping off his body, pooling underneath him before being pulled by gravity once again as it trickled off the rock and into the parched ground. Now fully out of the water, Wally grew hot within several moments but continued to lay flat, accepting the warm rays. He felt clean. He felt fresh. He felt ready to face whatever his future turned out to be.

―――

Andrew Bardin Williams is an author and brand strategist living in New Haven, Conn. His first novel, *Learning to Haight*, was named a finalist for the 2012 Indie Reader Discovery Award in literary fiction.

THANK YOU FOR READING!

Thank you! Thank you! Thank you! I hope you enjoyed Polk Gulch as much as I enjoyed writing it.

As you may know, independent authors survive on reviews. They are really the only way to level the playing field with the major publishing houses with unlimited resources. Please help by writing a review on Amazon and Goodreads, and, of course, spread the word to other readers who may enjoy being a fly on the wall during Wally's journey.

―――

In the meantime, check out the following sneak peek of my first book, *Learning to Haight*.

LEARNING TO HAIGHT

Jack and Dean tumbled out of the faded, weather-stained Victorian in San Francisco's Haight-Ashbury neighborhood on a Thursday afternoon, the streets still crowded with tourists and neighborhood types. It was what Jack liked to call a "Full House Day": sunny, cloudless, a perfect day to drive a shiny red convertible over the Golden Gate Bridge and hang out with Danny, Uncle Jesse, Kimmie Gibler and the Olsen twins.

Still high from the bud they'd smoked upstairs in Dean's apartment, they floated toward Ben & Jerry's scoop shop at the center of the hood, across the street from the famous Haight-Ashbury street sign. Dean, in a wrinkled white dress shirt, dusty jeans and no shoes, walked several feet ahead, his gangly legs taking long strides. Jack, two inches taller and forty-three years younger than his companion, was having considerable trouble keeping up with Dean's frenetic pace. Jack shoved his hands into his Lucky Brand jeans and let himself be pulled along behind, unwittingly drawn closer and closer into the Haight underworld, drafting in Dean's wake.

The pair reached the corner, and Dean paused to chat with a young couple crouched on the curb while Jack gasped to catch his breath, slouched against the side of the building in an attempt to support his quivering body.

An impromptu field trip was the last thing Jack had expected when, moments earlier, Dean had offered to show him the Sixties. Dean had been sitting cross-legged on the floor in his living room, waving a half-smoked joint in Jack's direction, urging him to break the rules. Jack carefully weighed the pros and cons of accepting the peace offering, conducting a quick cost-benefits analysis inside his head as Dean leaned in with the joint. Dean's broadening smile seemed to be tearing his face in half as Jack finally took the joint between his thumb and forefinger and took a gigantic hit.

Now, Jack stood outside on the corner of Haight and Ashbury, underneath a clock hanging over the sidewalk perpetually stuck on twenty past four, breathing heavily, watching Dean converse with the couple. Jack grinned, finally getting the 4:20 reference. His head swam as he watched Dean reach in his pocket, pull out a wad of bills and offer a few to the couple sitting on the corner.

"Thanks for the scratch," the man said, peering up from his nest of blankets laid out in front of the ice cream shop. He stuck out his long, sinewy arm, the malnourished muscles giving way to taut, exposed tendons. "We can eat this week."

When Dean smiled, dimples perfectly punctuated his shallow cheekbones. His once dark hair was now faded grey. His teeth were perfectly aligned but stained yellow from age, coffee and tobacco. Jack had learned that Dean had once been a handsome man, the darling of Hollywood, the next big thing, but those days were long gone, lost to a lifetime of what-ifs, drug binges and shifty associates. It wasn't for lack of opportunities. No, Dean had been front and center in some of the most important cultural events in San Francisco history, floating through life like a fly-on-the-wall as the Beat, Hippie and Hipster movements were born, flourished and eventually died. Jack had come to realize that Dean's problem wasn't proximity; rather, he seemed content to just be there, forgoing leadership roles to younger, more ambitious conspirators yet thriving in the afterglow of his more tuned in, media-savvy peers.

Regardless, Dean was an infamous figure in Haight-Ashbury. Born Henry Simmons to Armenian immigrants in California's Central Valley, Dean had later taken the name of his best friend, the iconic Fifties star James Dean, after the actor died in a car accident, tragically and much too young. The two had acted together in Rebel Without a Cause when Henry was simply an up-and-coming twenty-year-old actor with what could be described simply as It. The role, the only one of his career, was tiny and consisted of only a few lines. On the big screen he spoke his dialogue softly, confident in his California country accent--a dialect born from hillbilly surfers. He elongated his vowels and consistently dropped the 'g' in 'ing'. Man became maaaaan. Jumping became jumpin'. His line, "He's a hard-luck tramp if I ever seen one, eh Buzz? Who's he been runnin' with?" sent movie-goers bananas. Women wanted to be with him, men wanted to be him.

Albeit a small, insignificant role, Henry's immense screen

presence, classic good looks and off-screen chemistry with the film's stars set the studio executives buzzing, foreseeing a long and productive career for him in front of the camera. Henry had come along at the right time in the right movie, his role as a teenaged goon a burning memory in the minds of casting agents throughout Hollywood.

Just like fellow Rebel hoodlum Dennis Hopper, who actually did go on to have a successful movie career, Henry's part in the 1955 classic endeared him forever to an entire generation that recognized their own coming of age struggles in Post-War America.

Over the years, America's celebrity culture kept the newly christened Dean Simmons in the limelight, and those around him--leaders of various social movements and causes--sought to take advantage of his name and face, his constant need for attention. But Dean was no James. While the movie star was a natural leading man, Dean Simmons settled into the life of a sidekick, always a familiar face in the background, never up front and in charge.

Jack's head began to swim as he stared blindly at the conversation in front of him, watching mouths move but failing to hear the words spoken. The San Francisco June heat radiated off the sidewalk, causing sticky pools of sweat to collect and drip off the end of his jaw. He slowly sank to the ground, his shoulder keeping contact with the wall. First his knees touched the sidewalk, then his butt, finally the back of his head.

"Hey kid, you ok?" came a female voice next to him. Jack snapped out of his drug-induced daze and realized a woman was hovering above him. She must have been the wife or girlfriend of the man to which Dean had given the money. Her hair was dirty and matted but her eyes were wide, crystal clear, apparently immensely interested in the young man lying next to her on the sidewalk. "Whatcha doing? Taking a nap?"

Jack shook his head. "Just resting my eyes," he responded, waving the woman away. "Just resting my eyes."

The woman shrugged and turned her attention back to her boyfriend, who was still engaged in conversation with Dean, who had looked down at Jack still crumpled on the sidewalk. He extricated himself from the friendly banter and nudged Jack with his unshod foot. The black stained appendage came dangerously close to Jack's face, the smell of gym clothes, ashtray and street grime wafting under his nose.

"Ok, ok, I'm up," Jack said, sitting upright and wiping his eyes with the back of his hand. He struggled to his feet and stood gingerly next to Dean, swaying back and forth in his shoes. He ran his fingers through his short, black hair, pulling the strands taut, sending a wave of masochistic pleasure searing through his scalp. The extra minutes he spent that morning getting the perfect "bed head" look were now wasted, his carefully manicured 'do lost in a frizzy 'fro.

"Jack, time to move on," Dean declared. He firmly shook the hand of the man on the sidewalk and nodded goodbye. And with that, he bounded down the street in the direction of Golden Gate Park, Jack stumbling in his wake, his legs taking on a life of their own. He followed Dean past the head shops and T-shirt boutiques that lined Haight, grabbing hold of Dean's shirttail, his head on a swivel as they weaved in and out and around the masses lining the sidewalk, a puppy incessantly trying to smell every street sign and fire hydrant as he's being pulled along by his leash.

"Hey Dean, what's up, brotha'?" shouted a disheveled man lying slumped against the front of an organic food store with a Styrofoam cup at his feet, his face and hair smeared with dirt and grease. A young hipster in tight black jeans and a T-shirt emblazoned with the image of Che Guevara giving the finger stepped over the beggar as he exited the store. He paused as he recognized Dean, smiled broadly and stuck out his hand toward the local celebrity.

These, this crowd of miscreants, drifters, anti-heroes, were Dean's main constituents these days: strung-out, wannabe bohemian transients lured to the life by the promise of free love, cheap drugs and no responsibilities. They came looking for like-minded souls to share the streets. What they found was Dean, a familiar face and name, a man who understood them, galvanized them, helped them.

"You coming to the poetry reading at the People's Café tomorrow night? Janice Mirikitani will be performing new verses." Dean grasped the young hipster's hand and shook it vigorously. He looked Dean directly in the eyes and continued to pump his hand, apparently transfixed by the great man's presence while ignoring Jack who was still holding onto Dean's shirttail, the color of his knuckles starting to match his pale complexion. Dean managed to wriggle free without breaking stride and shouted back, "You know it, man. Wouldn't miss it for the world."

Jack glanced at the man in the Che T-shirt as he was pulled forward by Dean, noting an expression that beamed in Dean's wake, his silly grin never fading. He acted like he'd just touched Jesus. And in these parts, he pretty much had.

Dean seemed to know everyone in this funky, eclectic neighborhood, Jack thought, as he struggled to hold on and keep up. Back when the two ended up sharing that cab ride across town and hatched their plan for launching Jack off the news desk and onto the front page, he had seen Dean as a sympathetic figure, someone who had been shat upon, a hard-luck traveler who was given a shot but had it taken away. He could visualize the lead paragraph, right there on the front page, below the fold with a jump to page A-10: Dean Simmons has spent a lifetime fitting in, moving from movement to movement, constantly giving away a piece of himself to help those around him. Attention is his nourishment. His name is the only currency he needs.

He'd thought the story would write itself and the process would be painless, consisting of an hour or two with Dean who Jack would let babble on like he had the day they met. Jack's vision certainly did not include racing through the Haight, wasted off his ass, shaking hands with street people. But, then again, nothing had gone as expected since that fateful cab ride, and nothing, certainly not this fantastic journey on Dean's shirt tails, seemed that bizarre anymore. Despite this sidetrack, Jack was excited to get the opportunity to write his first feature for the San Francisco Daily Mirror, recognizing his chance meeting with Dean as fate.

Stepping over people lying on the sidewalk and sitting on the curb, Dean swam through the crowd, pulling Jack along behind him through a populace that was begging for money, selling drugs or simply enjoying the sunshine.

The Irish cops in Boston where Jack grew up would have never stood for this type of loitering, Jack thought, as he nearly tripped over a leg belonging to a woman selling figurines made from discarded wine corks. Stubby arms and legs protruded from the rotund cork bodies, reborn from discarded hangers found in a dumpster behind a local drycleaners. The paddy wagon would have cleaned up this neighborhood long ago, Jack thought, but perhaps this was why he had recently left the quaint colonial city for greener pastures out West. These people were unique individuals, free of pretension.

The duo reached the end of Haight Street, dead-ending at an entrance to Golden Gate Park. They left the crowded sidewalk, following a sloping asphalt path to an underpass and the gateway to the park. A group of young pot-heads wearing baggy jeans and hooded drug rugs sat in a circle on a patch of grass next to the tunnel and watched them as they passed.

"Green bud," one advertised, his penetrating eyes fixated squarely on the trailing passenger. Jack stuck close to Dean, turning his head in the other direction. He wasn't quite ready to alter his persona of the occasional user with friends-- undoubtedly a mooch--to become a cannabis connoisseur, one who actually purchased herb and hallucinogenic baked goods from people on the street. In contrast, Dean waved and smiled, receiving an earnest greeting in reply.

The two weren't half-way through the tunnel when the rhythmic beat reached them. Back in Dean's apartment, Jack had secretly hoped this was where they were going when Dean promised to "show him the Sixties." The hair stood up on the back of his neck as Dean quickened the pace, tugging him toward the concert. Up on a hill on the other side of a large grassy field, dozens of spectators lounged on blankets reading magazines, chatting or simply sitting and listening at the music being orchestrated in front of them. A group of twelve or fifteen collaborators held court, gathered around a park bench, hammering out a slow, rhythmic beat on an array of implements. Dean led Jack to the center of the crowd, plopping him down on the grass, high up on the hill, and focused his attention on the musicians below them.

Some members of the ragtag band of performers huddled around the weather-stained park bench and beat on a variety of percussion instruments--a set of bongo drums, a xylophone, a big bass drum more than three feet tall--but most improvised on other objects like an aluminum shopping cart, a plastic garbage can, the park bench itself. A particularly grungy-looking musician banged out a beat on a grey, water-stained tennis shoe that he held over his head, so lost in the beat, he didn't seem to notice his bare foot, stained black from walking the city streets, keeping rhythm in a murky puddle. The ringleader, a dreadlocked black man in an immaculately pressed three-piece suit, set the tone for the rest of the group, his long dreads whipping around as he nodded his head in time with the beat. His lips cried, "Yes!" over and over again as he changed the beat every few minutes, leading his disciples to serenity.

A wisp of fog rolled over the hedge of trees across the grassy field and streamed toward the concert, slowly swallowing the scores of kids in brightly-colored jerseys playing in a rec-league soccer game and their foul-mouthed parents yelling on the sidelines who secretly wished they themselves were playing. As the temperature began to drop, Jack remembered to pull on the fleece that had been tied around his waist throughout their adventure. Dean was in a trance, nodding his head to the music, repeating "Yes! Yes!" over and over again. Jack slipped off his shoes and leaned back, letting the grass tickle his ears. Closing his eyes, he concentrated on the music engulfing him, letting the sound overtake his consciousness.

———

Available now!

ALSO BY ANDREW WILLIAMS

Learning to Haight
Polk Gulch

ABOUT THE AUTHOR

Andrew Bardin Williams is an author and copywriter in New Haven, Connecticut. Inspired by the beats, Andrew strives to provide readers a sense of place in his fiction writing, using real-world locations to create setting, build tension, and develop character.

His first novel *Learning to Haight* was launched at the Beat Museum in San Francisco, named a finalist for the 2012 Indie Reader Discovery Award in literary fiction, and featured by www.kerouac.com and Dante's Hot Tub on Radio Valencia.

A new member of the New Haven arts community, Andrew is a participant in the "Get to the Point" storytelling series at Cafe Nine and has given a reading at the Institute Library. He is currently documenting the relationship between geography and literature through a grant from the Arts Council.

Connect with Andrew at andrewbardinwilliams.com.

Printed in Great Britain
by Amazon